MURDER IN THE GALLERY

An Augusta Peel Mystery Book 10

EMILY ORGAN

Copyright © 2025 by Emily Organ
All rights reserved.

emilyorgan.com

Emily Organ has asserted her right under the Copyright, Designs and Patents Act 1988 to be identified as the author of this work.

All characters and events in this publication, other than those clearly in the public domain, are fictitious and any resemblance to real persons, living or dead, is purely coincidental.

ISBN 978-1-7384465-8-2

This book is copyright material and must not be copied, reproduced, transferred, distributed, leased, licensed or publicly performed or used in any way except as specifically permitted in writing by the publisher, as allowed under the terms and conditions under which it was purchased or as strictly permitted by applicable copyright law. Any unauthorised distribution or use of this text may be a direct infringement of the author's and publisher's rights and those responsible may be liable in law accordingly.
This prohibition includes, but is not limited to, any reproduction or use for the purpose of training artificial intelligence technologies or systems.

The Augusta Peel Series

Death in Soho
Murder in the Air
The Bloomsbury Murder
The Tower Bridge Murder
Death in Westminster
Murder on the Thames
The Baker Street Murders
Death in Kensington
The Dockland Murder
Murder in the Gallery

Chapter One

A LOUD KNOCK jolted Augusta awake.

For a moment she lay still, heart thudding, unsure if she'd imagined it. Had it been real? Or just something from a dream?

Three sharp knocks followed.

With a groan, she reached for the bedside lamp. Harsh yellow light filled the room, and the clock's dial confirmed it was ten past two in the morning. Something must be wrong—surely no one called at this hour without reason. A fire? Trouble at the shop?

She pulled back the covers and shivered as she crossed the room and fetched her dressing gown from the hook on the door.

Again, three sharp knocks echoed through the flat.

'I'm coming!' she called out, her voice sharper than intended.

Barefoot on the cold linoleum, she padded to the front door and pressed her eye to the spy hole.

'Philip?' she said, startled. 'What is it?' Although she

felt pleased to see him, it was concerning that he was calling in the middle of the night. She feared the worst.

Hurriedly, she unfastened the chains and opened the door.

'I'm sorry for waking you, Augusta.' He leant in to give her a quick kiss but his expression remained serious. His overcoat smelled of damp wool and was spotted with raindrops. 'You need to get dressed and come with me.'

'What's happened?'

'I'll explain on the way. There's a car waiting outside.'

She frowned. 'Why won't you tell me now?'

'Because there's no time. He wants us to be quick.'

'*He?* Who are you talking about, Philip?'

'It will all become clear, but we need to leave.'

'You'd better come in while I change.'

'No it's alright, I'll see you downstairs, Augusta. It will take me a while to get down the steps.' He glanced down at his walking stick and gave her a smile.

'Of course. I'll see you shortly, Philip.'

Once she'd closed the door, she crossed her living room to the window and pulled back the curtain. Below, on Marchmont Street, a motor car idled with its headlamps glowing.

Who was in the car? Augusta hurried to her bedroom to dress.

Five minutes later, she joined Philip in the back of the waiting car. The interior smelled of pipe smoke. A man sat in the passenger seat beside the driver but it was too dark to see their faces. Augusta waited for them to introduce themselves. But they didn't.

'What's happening?' she asked over the noise of the

idling engine. 'Where are we going?' The lack of explanation unsettled her.

'We're going to the crime scene,' said the man in the passenger seat.

The car pulled away, heading south along Marchmont Street towards Russell Square. Augusta turned to Philip. She could barely make out his features in the dim light. 'What crime scene? Do you know where we're going?'

'No, I've no idea. They picked me up about twenty minutes ago. I haven't been told anything.'

She addressed the man in the passenger seat. 'Can I ask who you are?'

'All will be explained in due course, Mrs Peel. But I can assure you that there's no cause for alarm.'

Who was he and how did he know her name? She felt irritable about the lack of explanation.

'Well, it's reassuring there's no cause for alarm,' she said dryly. 'Being woken in the middle of the night and bundled into a car is hardly comforting.'

She leaned back in her seat and looked out of the window. The city was cloaked in darkness, the streets wet with rain. Only the occasional glow of a streetlamp lit the way, offering fleeting glimpses of shuttered shopfronts and silent buildings.

She stole glances at the men sitting in the front. Passing lights briefly illuminated them and revealed the man in the passenger seat wore glasses. Wisps of smoke curled from a pipe which the driver was smoking. There was a stiffness in the way the pair sat, as if they were bracing themselves for something unpleasant.

The voice of the man who'd spoken echoed in her mind. He'd said only a few words, but there was a familiarity she couldn't quite place.

The car made its way along New Oxford Street, then

Charing Cross Road. As they entered Trafalgar Square, it made a sudden right turn and stopped outside a large stone building—its classical façade marked by grand columns and a wide staircase leading to a pair of heavy double doors.

Augusta stared up at it in disbelief.

'The National Gallery?'

Chapter Two

THE MAN in the passenger seat was the first to get out. He didn't wait for them, nor did he look back. By the time Augusta had climbed from the car and closed the door behind her, he was already striding up the steps of the National Gallery with a bag in his hand, his silhouette almost lost in the rainy gloom.

'Who is he?' Augusta whispered to Philip as they followed.

'I don't know,' he murmured. 'But there's something about him... something familiar.'

'Yes!' Augusta felt a flicker of excitement stir in her stomach. 'That's exactly what I thought. I've seen him before.'

'It will come to us.'

They ascended the steps, Philip taking his time as he leant on his walking stick. Augusta kept close beside him, her breath misting in the night air. At the top of the steps, the man was waiting for them—still and silent, as if carved from the stone of the building itself.

'Is this where the crime scene is?' Augusta asked, unable to hold back her curiosity. 'In the gallery?'

'As I've said, Mrs Peel,' he replied, voice calm but guarded, 'all will become clear.'

'I've met you before, haven't I?' she pressed. 'You seem very familiar.'

'All in good time, Mrs Peel.'

Before she could respond, one of the great doors creaked open with a groan. A man stood there with a torch. 'There are three of you, then?'

The man confirmed this with a short nod, then stepped inside. Augusta and Philip followed.

The man with the torch wore a dark uniform with polished silver buttons and a cap. Augusta guessed he was a security guard. He led them swiftly through a succession of galleries, each room eerily hushed. The torchlight picked out glimpses of paintings in heavy gilt frames—Renaissance religious scenes, Dutch interiors, and brooding portraits with eyes which seemed to follow them through the dark. Augusta had visited the National Gallery many times, among the bustle of tourists and students. But tonight, under torchlight and silence, it felt like another world.

As they moved deeper into the building, the familiar galleries gave way to private areas: a corridor lined with closed doors, likely offices and storage rooms. They passed through another door, climbed a short staircase, and emerged into yet another corridor.

At last, they stopped before a door with a small brass plaque: "Curator, Provenance Research".

The nightwatchman remained in the hallway as the anonymous gentleman placed a gloved hand on the door handle. For the first time, he turned to face them.

Augusta was struck by a bolt of recognition. The thin,

ascetic face. The steel-grey eyes. The round, black-rimmed spectacles.

She had seen the face once before—in a smoky café on Tottenham Court Road, during the war. She'd answered a cryptic newspaper advertisement, walked into the café with a dozen questions, and walked out a member of British Intelligence.

'Mr Wetherell,' she breathed.

'Wetherell!' said Philip with sudden clarity. 'It's nice to see you again. It's been… what, several years now?'

Wetherell inclined his head politely. 'Too long.' He regarded them for a moment, his expression unreadable. 'You're both rather familiar with crime scenes,' he continued. 'In which case, I trust you won't be too disturbed by what you're about to see.'

With that, he pushed open the door.

Philip and Augusta exchanged a glance—then stepped inside.

Chapter Three

THE ROOM WAS AN OFFICE—QUIET, dim, and orderly. The bookshelves lining the walls were crammed with hardbound volumes and archival boxes. Three paintings rested on easels, their canvases partially shrouded by shadows. A single lamp on the large polished desk cast a pool of warm light, its glow illuminating the figure slumped on it.

A man was seated at the desk, his body folded forward, the side of his head resting motionless on a blotter. His face was a mottled red colour.

Augusta recoiled but remained calm. The man was clearly dead.

'This is Edward Galloway,' said Mr Wetherell quietly. He placed the leather bag he'd been carrying next to the doorway.

'The curator of provenance research?' said Philip.

'You know him?'

'No,' Philip replied, 'I'm just repeating what it says on the door.'

Wetherell regarded him for a moment. 'I think you may know him. Take a closer look.'

Augusta and Philip stepped toward the desk. The man's face was turned towards them. His eyes were closed and his expression slack. He had grey whiskers, and his hair was silvered with age.

Augusta hesitated, reluctant to approach any closer than necessary. Instead, she angled her head, adjusting her view to study his features.

Then she realised who he was.

His face was heavier than she remembered, the skin more lined, the jaw softened by time. But it was unmistakable. The years fell away as memories stirred, sharp and sudden.

'Jonathan Hastings,' she whispered.

'Hastings?' Philip moved closer. 'Goodness, you're right, Augusta. So it is. Our colleague in Belgium. I thought he was dead.'

'He is now,' said Wetherell dryly.

'But he was captured during the war wasn't he?' said Augusta. 'I didn't realise he survived. Like Philip, I assumed the worst had happened.'

Philip stepped back, looking around the room as if it might offer further context. 'So this is what he ended up doing—working as a curator at the National Gallery. That makes sense. He was a very talented artist.' He turned to Wetherell. 'What happened to him?'

'A few hours ago, the nightwatchman noticed a light coming from beneath the door. He knocked, received no response, and when he entered, this is what he found. At first, he assumed Galloway had fallen asleep.'

Augusta nodded slowly. 'He looks peaceful. It's not an unreasonable assumption.'

'He tried to wake him,' Wetherell continued, 'but quickly realised something was wrong. He telephoned the

Head of Security. And, wisely, the Head of Security called me.'

Philip's brow furrowed. 'Why you, Wetherell? Did they know his true identity here at the gallery?'

Wetherell shook his head. 'No. Mr Galloway—or rather, Hastings—called me a few weeks ago. He had concerns.'

'What sort of concerns?' Augusta asked.

'He'd received a letter. A threatening one. Someone out there knew who he really was. The sender didn't sign their name, but they clearly knew Galloway's wartime identity—his role, his background.'

'So he came to you?' said Augusta. 'For help?'

'Not help, exactly. He was never one to ask for that. He simply wanted me to be aware. To know that someone had found him. After our conversation, I had a quiet word with the Head of Security here at the gallery. I asked to be informed if anything unusual occurred.' Wetherell's gaze flicked to the body at the desk. 'When the call came this evening, I assumed it was another letter. I didn't expect this.'

'His death could be natural,' said Augusta. 'It may not have had anything to do with the letter.'

'Looking at the colour of his face, I'd say there's nothing natural about his death,' said Philip. 'That cherry-red appearance is a classic sign of cyanide poisoning. The question is, was it self-inflicted or did someone else do this to him?'

Wetherell nodded. 'I summoned a doctor to examine him and he confirmed the death is unexplained. He also suspects cyanide poisoning. There was a half-finished cup of coffee on the desk which has been taken away for examination. It's possible it could contain traces of cyanide.'

'What about the police?' asked Augusta.

'There's no need to involve them.'

'Why not?' asked Philip.

'Because Galloway's wartime identity has been compromised and it's possible his death is connected to it,' said Wetherell. 'No one at the Metropolitan Police can be allowed to get involved. Few of them have any idea how British Intelligence worked during the war and I'm concerned their clumsy efforts will uncover more identities which should remain secret.'

Philip bristled. 'They're not all hopeless at the Yard, I was there for a few years.'

'And you left because they made poor decisions,' said Wetherell. 'This is not a matter for the police. This is a matter for the secret service. You both worked for me once and I know I can trust you to manage this investigation with tact.'

'What about the doctor who examined Hastings?' said Philip. 'Isn't there a risk he'll talk?'

'I chose him carefully. He's a man I can trust. The death certificate will state that Edward Galloway died of cardiac arrest.'

Augusta's thoughts returned to Wetherell's words from a few moments previously. 'You want us to manage this investigation?' she asked him.

'Yes I want you to find out what happened to Galloway.'

'But why us?' Philip added. 'Just because we knew him?'

Wetherell gave a single nod. 'Exactly that.'

'But it's been years since we last saw him,' said Philip. 'I didn't even know he was working here.'

'It's been four years, Mr Fisher. Not a lifetime. And in that time, both of you have developed quite a reputation for uncovering the truth—particularly when the circumstances are... delicate.'

Augusta felt a flicker of unease. She hadn't realised Mr Wetherell had been keeping tabs on her work. The thought that someone from her past was still watching unsettled her.

'And what about your role in this?' Philip asked.

'My role is irrelevant,' Wetherell replied smoothly. 'In fact, it's better for all concerned if you don't mention you saw me here tonight.'

Philip narrowed his eyes. 'People will ask questions. His family and his colleagues when they arrive for work tomorrow.'

'Of course,' said Wetherell. 'That's all in hand. You needn't worry yourselves about that. So can I count on your complete discretion and cooperation?'

Augusta hesitated. 'It sounds like you're not giving us much choice, Mr Wetherell.'

'No choice at all,' Philip said bluntly. 'What happens if we refuse?'

Wetherell's expression didn't change. 'Are you saying you'd rather not be involved, Mr Fisher?'

'Yes,' Philip said evenly. 'Because I left British Intelligence when the war ended. I've spent the past four years at Scotland Yard, and now I work privately. I'm not under anyone's orders anymore—not yours, and not theirs.'

'You'll be remunerated, of course.'

'It's not about the money.'

Wetherell studied him. 'Then what is it about?'

'It's about being summoned here in the middle of the night and told, without explanation, that we're expected to investigate the suspicious death of a man we haven't seen in years. A man we barely knew outside of wartime service.'

'Yet you knew him,' Wetherell said simply. 'And that connection may be the key to understanding what happened here. The people who knew Hastings during the war are few—and some of them are already gone. I believe you both may be able to see what others can't.'

Philip looked to Augusta, as though waiting for her verdict. Like him, she felt irritated that they were being given little choice in the matter. However, she also wished to find out what had happened to Jonathan Hastings. How had he escaped capture during the war? And who had discovered his true identity?

She met Philip's gaze and gave a small nod.

'Very well,' he said to Wetherell. 'We'll look into it.'

A faint smile touched Wetherell's lips. 'That's all I ask.' He gestured to the leather bag he'd left by the doorway. 'You'll find some things in there that should prove useful— a magnifying glass, a basic fingerprint kit, and so on. An undertaker is arriving to collect the body at three o'clock and you'll want to be finished by then.' He checked his watch. 'It's a quarter to two now so you don't have long, I'm afraid. Good luck, and I look forward to hearing your findings.'

He turned to leave.

'And if we have questions?' Philip asked.

Wetherell paused at the door. 'You're a capable investigator, Mr Fisher. I trust you'll find your own way to the answers. That said, should I receive further information, I'll ensure it reaches you. I'll send you the results of the postmortem once they're available.'

He reached for the handle, then looked over his shoulder. 'And please don't attempt to contact me in Whitehall —they don't know me by my name there.'

With that, he slipped through the door and was gone.

Chapter Four

PHILIP AND AUGUSTA stood in silence for a moment. They exchanged a glance—part disbelief, part resignation.

'So we don't have a choice,' Philip muttered, rubbing the back of his neck. 'I've no idea what the consequences would be for turning this down, but I suspect they'd be unpleasant.'

Augusta looked at the desk and the lifeless form slumped on it. 'Well,' she said quietly, 'I must admit I'm curious. I don't care for Mr Wetherell's tactics, but I want to know what happened to Hastings. The last time I saw him, he was painting a pretty view of Lac du Corbeau.'

'A painting which would have concealed a hidden map within its brushstrokes,' added Philip. 'I can't say I cared much for Hastings as a gentleman, but there's no denying he had a talent.'

Augusta glanced at the corpse and recalled the man she'd known during wartime. Hastings had been self-assured and confident in his abilities. Confident to the point of arrogance. She recalled a man who'd been quick to impress and slow to listen, proud but often oblivious to the effect his actions had on others.

'I don't think he had the right character to be an agent,' she said. 'But there's little doubt he was good at what he did. The paintings he made in Belgium and sent back to England informed several successful missions.'

'True,' agreed Philip. 'I always held a grudging respect for the man. I can't say I liked him much and I don't even feel guilty saying that now he's deceased. He made a lot of enemies.'

A pause followed and names and faces from the past ran through Augusta's mind.

'But we don't have time to consider all that now,' added Philip. 'We need to be out of here before the undertaker arrives at three, so we need to get on.' He stepped over to the leather bag and opened it. He took out two pairs of gloves and handed a pair to Augusta. 'I'm going to have a closer look at his corpse,' he said.

'And I'll happily leave you to that,' said Augusta, putting on her gloves. 'I'll look around the room.'

She stepped over to the three paintings. The one which caught her eye first was a portrait of muted tones depicting a sombre woman in mourning attire. Her dress looked medieval. She was painted from the waist up and held a bird in one hand. Her dark glassy eyes were fixed on something distant to her right.

Another painting was a bright landscape with a flowery meadow, verdant trees and gentle rolling hills in the distance. For a brief moment, it transported Augusta to a summer's day in the countryside. She could almost hear the birdsong and feel the warm sunlight on her face.

The third painting was a still life arrangement. Augusta peered closely at the fruit and flowers and was impressed by their detail, but the overall picture interested her little.

Instead, she felt herself drawn back to the sombre woman with the bird. There was a brightness in the little creature's eye which contrasted sharply with the deadened stare of the lady who held it.

'How are you getting on?' Philip asked her.

'Just looking at the paintings,' said Augusta.

'Any clues?'

'No.'

'We only have an hour.'

'I know. I don't need reminding.' She moved away from the paintings and turned to the bookshelves. Taking down one of the archival boxes, she placed it on a table and began looking through its contents. She yawned and remembered she'd only had two hours of sleep. Somehow she would have to spend a day working in her bookshop after this. The work was tiring and Augusta felt uncomfortable sharing a room with Hastings' corpse.

Despite this, she felt the familiar pull of the unknown —a mixture of duty, intrigue, and the thrill of chasing the truth.

Chapter Five

'Well, this is sad news,' said Augusta's assistant, Fred, as he read the newspaper at the bookshop counter later that morning. 'A curator at the National Gallery was found dead in his office last night. Apparently he died of a sudden heart attack.'

'That is sad,' Augusta replied. She liked and trusted Fred. He'd been a steady ally over the past year, always observant, always dependable. She hated keeping a secret from him, but it wasn't her choice. Not yet.

She stifled a yawn as she fed Sparky some birdseed. The little canary hopped about excitedly in his cage on the counter.

'I hope you don't mind me saying so but you look tired, Augusta,' said Fred.

'Yes I didn't sleep very well,' she replied through another yawn. Her head ached and her eyes felt sore. No matter what she occupied herself with, an image of Hastings' mottled red face kept entering her mind. She wished now Wetherell had never called on her and Philip to investigate the unexplained death.

'If you want to get some rest, I can look after the shop,' he said.

'Really, Fred? That's very kind of you. I think I'll take you up on your offer. If I can get an hour's rest then I think I shall be alright for the rest of the day. Do you think you'll be alright looking after Sparky and the bookshop.'

Fred grinned. 'I think I can manage it.'

Augusta was just about to fetch her bag and walk the short distance back to her flat when the bell above the shop door chimed. Its cheerful note was at odds with the troubled expression of Lady Hereford, who entered being pushed in her bath chair by her nurse. Her face was tight with distress, her eyes wide and unsettled.

Augusta immediately felt a flicker of concern. 'Lady Hereford, whatever is the matter?' she asked.

The nurse wheeled the chair up to the counter. Lady Hereford gripped the armrests with white-knuckled hands. 'I don't think I can endure another night at the Russell Hotel,' she declared. Her voice, although firm, carried a tremor beneath it.

'But it's your home.' Lady Hereford had lived in a suite at the Russell Hotel ever since she'd left hospital the previous year. After selling her large, costly house, the hotel had become a manageable, comfortable solution.

'It *was* my home,' the old lady corrected sharply. 'But I cannot—will not—share it with *that* woman.'

Augusta frowned, puzzled. 'Which woman?'

'The Dowager Lady Pontypool. Can you believe it? She's taken the suite next door to mine! She arrived three days ago.'

'I'm afraid I don't recall the name,' Augusta admitted. 'Who is she?'

Lady Hereford's eyebrows shot up. 'Have I truly never mentioned her? We had a dreadful falling out at our debutante ball.' She waved a gloved hand as if brushing away decades. 'She was Rosemary Blenkinsop then. We were waiting in line to be presented to the Queen. In the shuffle, I accidentally stepped on her train and put my foot through it. The tear was barely noticeable, I assure you. But the fuss she made!'

'Oh dear,' said Augusta.

'She shrieked like a wounded peacock,' Lady Hereford continued. 'You'd think I'd ruined the entire Season. And it was a tear you could barely notice. The Queen certainly wasn't looking at hems.' She sniffed. 'Her Majesty appeared rather disinterested that entire evening.'

'So Lady Pontypool never forgave you?'

'Never. She's made it her mission to remind me of that incident at every social gathering we've both attended since. Christenings. Weddings. Funerals. No matter the occasion, there she is—ready with some barbed comment or cutting remark.' The old lady scowled. 'And now, after all these years, she's moved onto my floor at the Russell. As if she's haunting me! And she's brought a dog with her. A ghastly creature. Yaps incessantly. I believe it's a Pomeranian, although it resembles a badly mended cushion.'

Augusta chuckled despite the serious tone. 'I'm sorry you have to endure her company again. But surely you wouldn't let her drive you from your home? You've been so content at the Russell Hotel. You've said yourself that the staff are attentive and the location is ideal.'

Lady Hereford sighed heavily. 'I have been happy there. But I can't be happy there any longer. Not when I know our paths are likely to cross at any moment.' She adjusted the fur around her shoulders, as if bracing herself for battle.

'Perhaps age has mellowed her,' Augusta suggested.

'Age mellows the gracious, not the venomous,' Lady

Hereford responded tartly. 'And Rosemary has always been the latter. You'll see for yourself soon enough.' She turned to the canary in his cage. 'I thought I would cheer myself up by calling on you—and Sparky.' She addressed the canary. 'How are you today, Sparky? Any unwelcome neighbours?'

'No,' Augusta smiled. 'Sparky gets along with everyone.'

'So do I!' Lady Hereford protested, lifting her chin. 'It's the Dowager Lady Pontypool who doesn't get along with me.'

Suppressing a chuckle, Augusta handed the bag of birdseed to Lady Hereford, sensing that a little time spent fussing over the canary might settle her frayed nerves.

Sure enough, after a few moments, the old lady's brow began to soften. 'Doesn't he keep himself in wonderful condition?' she remarked, feeding the seeds carefully through the bars. 'He preens so beautifully. His feathers are immaculate, aren't they, Augusta?'

'Yes, they are. Remarkable really, when you think he has only his beak to manage it all.'

'Quite a wonder, this little fellow.' Lady Hereford's voice had taken on a gentler, almost wistful tone. She continued to watch Sparky for a moment, then turned her sharp gaze back to Augusta. 'And how are you, my dear? Any intriguing cases at the moment?'

Augusta hesitated. She longed to confide in Lady Hereford—to share the complexities and dangers of the Edward Galloway investigation.

'No investigations at the moment,' Augusta replied, forcing a light tone. 'Which gives me a bit more time to repair the stack of books piled up in the workshop.' She smiled. 'Although Fred has been doing a very fine job himself lately.'

'Excellent. You're training him up properly, then?'

'Yes, very well. He's got quite the knack for it. I'll put the kettle on, shall I?'

'That would be lovely.'

Augusta felt the weight of the unspoken words between them. Lady Hereford had always been a confidante—wise, perceptive, and trustworthy. It felt unnatural to keep things from her.

As she prepared the tea, Augusta promised herself that when the truth about Edward Galloway had been uncovered, she would tell Fred and Lady Hereford everything.

Chapter Six

AFTER LADY HEREFORD HAD DEPARTED, Philip descended the stairs from his office.

'I got back from lunch to find this envelope on my desk,' he said, holding it up. 'You didn't happen to see who left it, did you?'

'I didn't see anyone at all,' Augusta said.

'Wetherell must have slipped in unnoticed. Either that, or he sent one of his shadows to deliver it. Shall we see what he's sent us?'

Upstairs in his office, they sat in two easy chairs with a small table between them. Philip opened the envelope and pulled out the papers. He placed them on the table and picked up the document on top of the pile. His brow creased as he scanned the first page.

'This is the attending doctor's report,' he said, voice low. 'It says Hasting's death was sudden and unexplained. The doctor thinks he died some time between eight o'clock and ten o'clock yesterday evening.' He picked up the next set of documents. 'And here we have the postmortem report. It appears to confirm Hastings' death was caused by cyanide poisoning.'

Augusta pulled a grimace. She'd heard about suffering endured in cases of cyanide poisoning, the only consolation was that it was short-lived before death. 'So the question is, did he take the cyanide deliberately?' she asked.

'This report doesn't say,' said Philip, looking through the pages.

'It probably won't say on the post mortem report.' Augusta picked up the papers from the table. 'It will be in a separate report. Wetherell told us the coffee cup and its contents were being examined… Here we are, "Medico-Legal Toxicology Report".'

'Well done, Augusta. What does it say?'

'"The contents of the coffee cup contained a notable quantity of hydrocyanic acid—cyanide. The level detected, approximately eight grains per fluid ounce, is sufficient to prove fatal if ingested in full. The average adult lethal dose is estimated at two to five grains."'

'Goodness,' said Philip, sitting back in his chair. 'I can't imagine he inflicted that upon himself.'

'Me neither,' replied Augusta. 'The report concludes, "It is the opinion of the undersigned that the substance was added post-brewing." It appears to be quite simple. Someone put that cyanide in his cup of coffee.' She sighed. 'He would've suffered.'

'He would,' Philip said softly. 'It's a particularly vicious poison. Not a kind way to go.'

A silence settled between them as they absorbed the weight of it. Outside, a bus rumbled past, the ordinary noise jarring with the darkness of their conversation.

'So we need to find out who poisoned Hastings. And when.'

Philip put the papers down on the table. 'Precisely. But

here's the problem—apart from Wetherell and his medical chaps, we're the only ones who know this was a murder. The coroner will give his cause of death as a heart attack.'

'And if everyone believes Hastings—or Galloway as they knew him—died of natural causes, we won't get far walking into the National Gallery and asking questions.'

'No, we won't,' said Philip. 'Which means we'll need a reason to speak to people. A convincing one.'

Chapter Seven

'WE COULD PRETEND to be friends of his,' said Augusta. 'It's not too far from the truth because we worked with him in Belgium.'

'Yes I think friends could be a good cover for our work. I never felt I got to know him, though. He didn't give much away, did he? I suppose none of us did because information could be dangerous during those times. But of all the people we worked with, I felt Hastings was the one I knew least about. He was a private man.'

'I didn't really know him either,' said Augusta. 'He was a prickly sort of man. But he was good at his job. His paintings were remarkable not only for his talent but the information he hid within them. The Germans believed he was just a Belgian artist, painting for fun.'

'I never thought I'd see him again,' added Philip. 'And I suppose I didn't—not while he was alive, anyway. I just assumed he was one of the ones we lost.'

They both fell quiet, the unspoken names of lost colleagues casting a shadow.

Augusta broke the silence. 'I wonder how Hastings

escaped,' she said quietly. It had been widely whispered during the war that Hastings was captured by the enemy.

'He must have talked his way out,' said Philip. 'He would have been good at that. Perhaps the Germans didn't realise he was a British spy. He was a very convincing Belgian artist so maybe he continued to fool them. We'll never know for sure. Some secrets stay buried. I imagine Wetherell knows.'

'And if he does,' said Augusta, 'there's no chance of him telling us, is there?'

'Perhaps not,' said Philip. 'But let's see what else we have here.' He leaned forward and leafed through the papers on the table. 'Look, Wetherell's included a profile. It says here Hastings was fifty-three, widowed and lived alone in Wandsworth. He leaves a daughter, twenty-two. Her name is Lillian Galloway.'

'A daughter?' Augusta felt a pang of sympathy. 'And she'll have no idea her father was murdered. What about the rest of his background?'

'He's been working at the National Gallery for four years. Before then, he was supposedly employed at an art gallery in Canada.'

She gave a smile. 'Which we both know is fiction.'

'Of course,' Philip said. 'That covers his wartime activities, I imagine. The gallery in Canada was likely a convenient fabrication. Here's some information on his early life. Born in Dorset, educated at Millfield School. His father was an art dealer. And he was the third of five children. He had two brothers and two sisters. He studied the history of art at Oxford then completed a degree at the Slade School of Fine Art.' He turned the piece of paper and appeared disappointed it was blank on the other side. 'And that's all we have,' he added.

'I didn't know any of that about him,' said Augusta.

'But we didn't talk about our personal lives in Belgium, did we?'

'No, there was no call for it. We had to concentrate on our work.'

Augusta reached for another document which was handwritten. 'Two names have been written here,' she said. 'Some hurried notes of Wetherell's perhaps. "Vanessa Curwen, art dealer and Cecil White-Thomas, National Gallery."'

Philip's eyes narrowed. 'Interesting. I wonder if these are Wetherell's suspects?'

'He's clearly pointed us in their direction for a reason. At the very least, they were close enough to Hastings that they might know something.'

She laid the paper down. 'We'll need to meet with each of them. And we'll have to stay in character.'

Philip sat back. 'I can be Roger.'

'Roger?'

'Edward Galloway's old friend. And you can be my wife, Amelia.'

'Am I a friend of Edward's too?'

'Sort of. You knew him through my relationship with him.'

'And when did we last see him?'

'A long time ago. Two years even. We don't want to have seen him recently because his real friends and family may wonder why they've never heard of us at all.'

'So we're his long-lost friend and wife?'

'That's right. Mr and Mrs Parker.'

'Parker?'

'Yes,' said Philip. 'Does that sound alright? We want an ordinary name. Nothing too memorable. We don't want to stand out. In fact, the blander we can be, the better.'

'Roger and Amelia Parker,' said Augusta. 'It sounds alright to me.'

'Good.'

'And I suppose I'll discover what it's like to be married to you, Philip.'

Her remark caught him off-guard. 'Really?' He blushed a little then rubbed the back of his neck. 'Well, not quite. This is all just pretend, isn't it? I don't want it to affect our actual relationship, Augusta. We have to make a clear distinction between our professional relationship and personal one.'

Augusta smiled. 'I realise that. I was only making a joke.'

'Oh a joke? Yes, well I knew that really…' He rubbed his neck again. 'Anyway. No talk of marriage at the moment please. I am, after all, still married to Audrey even though we're estranged.'

Augusta felt a bitter taste in her mouth. She didn't like being reminded about Philip's wife. She picked up the papers, straightened them and pushed them back into the envelope.

Philip seemed to notice the change in her mood. 'So shall we visit the National Gallery again tomorrow?' he said brightly. 'Let's speak to some people there and see what they can tell us about Hastings.'

Augusta nodded. 'But whatever you do, don't accidentally call him Hastings. Otherwise we'll blow our cover before we've even got started.'

Chapter Eight

THE SIGN on Cecil White-Thomas's door stated he was the Chief Conservator of Paintings at the National Gallery.

In his warm, book-lined office a cheerful fire crackled behind the brass grate and a dark oil painting hung above the fireplace.

Mr White-Thomas was a tall, lean man with high cheekbones and a sharp jawline. Behind his spectacles, his pale, hooded eyes held an imperious gaze which gave the impression he was used to being listened to—and rarely challenged. He wore a sage green tweed suit with a tangerine silk handkerchief folded in his breast pocket. He gestured courteously to a pair of chairs facing him. 'Please, do sit down.'

'Thank you for agreeing to see me,' said Philip, lowering himself into the seat beside Augusta. 'I'm Roger Parker, an old friend of Edward Galloway and this is my wife Amelia.' Augusta gave a gracious nod. 'As soon as I heard the dreadful news about Edward I felt I had to come to London and speak to those who knew him. I hope you don't mind.'

He dabbed at his forehead with a handkerchief. Augusta, watching him from the corner of her eye, thought he was doing an excellent job of appearing shaken.

'Please accept my condolences,' said Mr White-Thomas, adjusting his spectacles. 'Edward was a dear colleague of mine for four years. I shall miss him greatly.'

The words were appropriate, yet there was something studied about his delivery. Augusta detected no genuine warmth, no flicker of grief.

'Can you believe I hadn't seen him for two years?' said Philip with a sigh. 'I should have made more effort. We were very close, once. I regret terribly not coming to London to see him while I still could.'

Mr White-Thomas nodded in solemn agreement. 'Yes, I understand. Life has a way of moving faster than we expect. We all have good intentions—letters to write, visits to arrange. But somehow, the days slip by, don't they? And before we realise it, the opportunity is lost.'

'Indeed,' Philip murmured. 'The manner of his death... it was just so sudden. I still can't quite believe it's true.'

'Quite. I was just as shocked as you are, Mr Parker.'

'Did you see him on the day he died?'

'I did. We spoke about a Monet which the gallery is about to receive on loan from the Louvre. There was some lively discussion over which gallery it should hang in when it arrives. The discussion was quite heated actually.' He gave a brief, humourless chuckle. 'So we agreed to disagree, and said we'd return to the conversation later. Sadly, that won't be possible now. I still can't quite believe he's gone.' He shook his head. 'In fact, it seemed to me that he was in perfect health. He always looked after himself. Regular walks and no over-indulgence. I suppose his heart must have failed him without warning. These things can be silent until it's too late, I suppose.' He gave a sniff. 'A very cruel tragedy.'

'Did you get on well with him?' Philip asked.

'Of course. We had our differences, but only professional ones and we had respect for one another's expertise. Edward never hesitated to challenge a view—and I respected that. It kept things... interesting. We weren't friends in the personal sense—our temperaments were rather different—but he was the sort of man you could rely on. A steady, reasoned voice. One of the few people here I'd trust for an honest opinion.'

'Yes, indeed,' Philip said with a wistful nod. 'He was full of sensible advice.'

'And it had been two years since you last saw him?'

Philip nodded. 'We corresponded frequently, though. He was a prolific letter writer—his notes were like essays, full of analysis and commentary. Always something to mull over.'

Mr White-Thomas smiled faintly. 'Oh yes, that sounds like Edward. A man who took his thoughts seriously. And he expected others to do the same. Our discussions here were often... thorough.'

He leaned back in his chair, steepling his fingers. The firelight played across the glass of his spectacles, briefly obscuring his eyes. Augusta couldn't help but wonder what he was thinking.

'I do wish I had more personal memories to offer you,' he continued. 'But I'm afraid most of my acquaintance with Edward was professional. No shared holidays, no dinner parties, nothing of that sort.'

'That's quite all right,' said Philip. 'Any recollection is appreciated.'

There was a short silence. Outside, rain pattered softly

against the tall windows. In the stillness of the room, Augusta felt the first stirrings of unease.

Philip spoke next. 'Would it be too much of an imposition to visit my late friend's office?'

'I don't see why not,' said Mr White-Thomas. 'I'll ask Miss Miller if she can show you in. She was Edward's secretary.' He pressed a button on his desk and his secretary stepped in through the door. 'Fetch Georgina Miller would you please, Miss Caterham.'

A few minutes later, a petite, fair-haired lady arrived. She wore a simple black blouse and skirt—mourning attire, Augusta noted. Her face was pale and composed, but her eyes were faintly rimmed with pink.

'Miss Miller,' said Mr White-Thomas, rising to his feet, 'this is Mr and Mrs Parker. Mr Parker was a close friend of Edward's. He'd very much like to see his office, if that's possible.'

'Of course,' she said quietly. 'I'd be more than happy to show you.' She gave them a small, polite smile. 'Follow me.'

They stepped into the corridor behind her. The parquet floor creaked faintly beneath their feet and Augusta reminded herself she had to appear unfamiliar with where they were going. She kept her expression composed, her eyes resting casually on the walls as though seeing them for the first time.

Miss Miller paused outside the door with the sign reading "Curator, Provenance Research", and fitted a key into the lock. She hesitated for a brief moment before turning it and pushing the door open.

Philip and Augusta stepped inside.

The room had the close, still feel of a place recently sealed. The air was slightly musty. Papers lay neatly stacked on the desk, and a jacket still hung on the back of

Galloway's chair, as though he might return at any moment.

Augusta glanced around. The room was the same as they'd left it early the previous morning. But there was one noticeable difference. One of the three paintings which had been resting on easels had vanished.

Only two paintings remained.

Chapter Nine

AUGUSTA INSTINCTIVELY LOOKED to Philip to see if he'd noticed the missing painting. But he was too deep in character, drawing in a shaky breath and staring at the desk.

'Is this where... where he was found?' he asked quietly.

Georgina Miller nodded, her lips pressing together. 'Yes. They said he died at his desk. He'd been working late —as usual. He often did.'

'It must have been very sudden indeed,' said Philip.

'I hope it was,' she replied. Her voice wavered slightly. 'I can't bear the thought of him suffering. I like to think it was quick. Peaceful. That he didn't feel a thing.'

Philip gave her a moment, then asked gently, 'How long did you work for him?'

'Three months. I began working here at the gallery just under a year ago. After a while I was asked to be Mr Galloway's secretary.'

'And you got on well?'

'Extremely well,' she said, her voice brightening slightly. 'He was a very clever man. Very kind. And so talented—not just as an art historian, but as an artist too.'

Augusta smiled at the memory of the sketches she'd seen Hastings make during the war.

'Did he still paint?' Philip asked.

'Oh yes,' Miss Miller said, nodding. 'Quite often, in fact. He didn't talk about it much, but I knew he painted in his spare time. He was shy about people seeing his work, but one day I asked if he'd show me what he'd been working on.'

'And did he?'

'He did,' she replied with a hint of a smile. 'He brought in a few rolled-up canvases. The paintings were beautiful. I told him he should consider holding an exhibition—he had the connections, of course. But he was reluctant. He said it wasn't the right time. I think he would have come around to it, eventually...' Her voice trailed off. She turned to look at his empty chair with the jacket on the back. Her hand rested lightly on the edge of the desk and Augusta noticed her nails were short and rough, as if regularly bitten. 'It's strange,' Miss Miller said softly, almost to herself. 'Even now, I half expect him to walk back in, carrying a book or humming under his breath. And to be in this room without him here… It doesn't feel real.'

No one spoke for a moment. The room was quiet, save for the faint tick of a clock on the mantelpiece.

Philip cleared his throat. 'Thank you,' he said gently. 'It means a great deal, hearing these things. He was lucky to have someone like you here.'

Miss Miller gave a small nod. 'We were all lucky to know him.' She glanced around the room and her eyes rested on the two pictures. 'I'm sure there was another painting when I was last in here.'

'Really?' Philip looked around, as if surprised to hear this. 'Where?'

'Just there.' She nodded at the pictures on the two

easels. There was a gap between them where the painting and its easel had stood.

'When were you last in here?' Augusta asked her.

'Yesterday morning when I first heard what had happened. I was told they'd taken him away during the night and I wanted to come in and see his room. The painting was there then.'

'Which painting was it?' Philip asked.

'It's called *Portrait of a Widow with a Lark*. By the artist Veridiano.'

Augusta recalled the painting of the sombre woman with a bird in her hand.

'Veridiano?' said Philip. 'I've not heard of him. Is it a valuable painting?'

'I believe so. He's the Renaissance artist who's been recently rediscovered. There's been a lot of excitement about his work.'

This remark piqued Augusta's interest. A popular missing artwork and Hastings' death. Could there be a connection? She tried to quell the excitement bubbling in her chest. As the supposed wife of a pretend friend of Galloway's, she couldn't display too much curiosity.

'And you're quite sure about this?' Philip asked Miss Miller. 'You think a painting has been removed since yesterday morning?'

'Yes,' she said. 'I shall ask around and find out who moved it. It seems odd that someone would take it from here so soon after his death. It seems disrespectful somehow. He was working on that painting and establishing its provenance.'

'He wanted to be certain it was painted by Veridiano?' asked Augusta.

Miss Miller nodded. 'That's right. It's a lot of work, as you can imagine. He was examining the media and the style. And he was also carrying out a lot of research to establish where it had been for the past four hundred years.'

'Not an easy task,' said Philip.

'No. But he was very clever at that sort of thing.' She scratched her chin. 'I'll check the storage rooms. It's possible someone's put it in one of those for safekeeping.'

'Good idea,' said Augusta.

'Do you mind me asking when you last saw my friend Edward?' Philip asked Miss Miller.

'Well it was in here on the evening he died,' she said, sadly. 'He often worked late into the evening. He enjoyed his work—lived for it, really. He didn't have anyone waiting at home. His wife passed away some years ago, and I think the quiet of this place at night suited him. He preferred staying on, rather than sitting alone in his flat.' She paused and took out a handkerchief from her pocket. 'I finished my work at half past five, as I usually do. I came in here and asked him if he needed me to do anything else. That was something I did every evening before leaving. He told me I could go and I said goodnight and that was the last time I saw him.' Her voice choked a little but she continued. 'I went home, had my evening meal, then called on my sister and her husband. Just an ordinary evening, nothing special. And to think... while I was laughing and chatting with them, he might have been here—suffering...' A sob interrupted her and she brought her handkerchief to her eyes.

Augusta stepped over to her and rested a hand on her arm. She barely knew the woman but she wanted to give her some comfort.

'If it had happened earlier,' continued Miss Miller through sobs, 'while I was still here... perhaps I could have done something. Maybe he cried out. Maybe he tried to reach the door. I keep thinking about it—what if I'd stayed just a little longer?'

'You weren't to know,' said Augusta, softly. 'No one could have predicted what happened. It was sudden and unexpected and you did all you could.'

Miss Miller nodded and wiped her eyes. 'Thank you, Mrs Parker. And I'm sorry. You must be just as upset as I am and here I am crying in front of you!'

Chapter Ten

AFTER LEAVING THE NATIONAL GALLERY, Augusta and Philip had a cup of tea in the Lyons Corner House just off Leicester Square. Lively chatter, clinking teacups and the smell of damp clothing surrounded them. Waitresses in their distinctive black and white uniforms bustled efficiently around the countless tables.

'Whenever I come to a Corner House, I wish I'd chosen somewhere smaller and quieter,' said Philip. He sipped his tea with a scowl.

'There's a reason we come here,' said Augusta. 'You know what you're getting. The service is always good and so is the tea. I prefer smaller places too. Some are good and some are less so.'

Philip placed his cup in his saucer. 'So what did you make of Cecil White-Thomas, Augusta?'

'I found him rather typical for a gentleman of his position. He's well-mannered and confidently pleased with himself.'

Philip smiled. 'Smug, you mean?'

'Yes I suppose so. And he was extremely tactful about

his relationship with Edward Galloway. He admitted they had occasional disagreements, then reassured us that was nothing to worry about.'

'So he's partly admitting they didn't get on, you think?'

'Yes I think so.'

'If only we'd spoken to him after we visited Galloway's office. We could have asked him if he knew anything about the missing painting.'

'If he did, he probably wouldn't be honest about it,' said Augusta.

'You think he'd lie?'

'Of course. I didn't like him much at all so at the moment I think he's capable of anything.'

Philip raised an eyebrow. 'Goodness. I was prepared to be a little more charitable about the chap. But I trust your instincts, Augusta, so I'll put his name down as a suspect.' Philip pulled his notebook and pen from his inside pocket. 'And what about Georgina Miller? She was Galloway's secretary and presumably made his coffee for him.

'She told us she left at half past five and it's believed Galloway died some time between eight o'clock and ten o'clock.'

'She could have made the cup of coffee for him before she left and he was so involved with his work that he forgot and drank it cold later that evening.' Philip pulled a grimace. 'That wouldn't have been very nice. A cold cup of cyanide coffee.'

'And I think it's unlikely,' said Augusta. 'He must have made himself that cup of coffee.'

'So how did someone else put cyanide in it?'

'It would have been someone who visited his office that evening. It could have been Miss Miller but she told us she called on her sister so she has a possible alibi.'

Philip sat back in his chair. 'White-Thomas could have

called on him, couldn't he? We need to find out what time White-Thomas left the gallery that evening.'

'We could ask him outright if we weren't working undercover,' said Augusta. 'But it's not the sort of question Edward Galloway's long-lost friend would ask.'

'No it isn't.' Philip scratched his chin. 'We're quite constrained when working undercover. We need answers, but we can't afford to draw attention to ourselves. What I find most peculiar is the absence of the police. If there were a proper investigation, a detective could walk into the gallery and start asking questions without having to tiptoe around anyone.'

'But as far as everyone else is concerned,' said Augusta, 'Edward Galloway died of natural causes. A heart attack. And that leaves us as the only ones asking questions. While pretending that we're not.' She picked up her teaspoon and stirred her tea as she thought. 'It's interesting that Georgina Miller noticed the missing painting too. Was Galloway murdered so the painting could be stolen from his office?'

'In which case, why wasn't it taken by the murderer at the time?' said Philip. 'The culprit could have ripped it out of its frame and taken off. I think the explanation could be simple. As Miss Miller suggests, perhaps someone moved it to a storage room for safekeeping. If the artist Verandi... no, Veridna... er, what was it again?'

'Veridiano.'

'Yes, him. Well remembered, Augusta. If Veridiano is a prized artist then his work will be worth a lot.'

'Miss Miller said he'd been rediscovered. Presumably that means he was forgotten about for a few centuries until someone came across his paintings again.'

'Yes, that suggests so. I'm only guessing though. Everything I know about art could be written on the back of this serviette here. And there'd still be room for the tea stain.'

Augusta laughed. 'I can't say my knowledge of art is much better. But I have a feeling that you and I are going to have to learn about it quite quickly.'

Philip consulted his notebook. 'We have another name which Wetherell has given us. Vanessa Curwen, an art dealer. Let's look her up in the directory and pay her a visit tomorrow.'

Chapter Eleven

'How was your day, Cecil?' his wife asked as the maid placed a steaming bowl of onion soup before him.

'Rather strange,' he said, draining his sherry. 'It feels... odd. The atmosphere at the gallery has changed completely. With Edward gone, it's as though something essential has been cut away.'

He picked up his spoon and stirred the soup absently before taking a mouthful.

'Yes, I expect it is odd,' said Margaret, unfolding her serviette with deliberate grace and settling it in her lap. 'It's not every day someone drops dead at their desk. What on earth was he doing there, working so late?'

'We all work late, Margaret,' Cecil replied. 'His work was his life. You know that.'

'Yes, I do,' she said. 'But it's rather sad, isn't it? To have no one waiting at home, so you just... stay in your office all evening. There's something terribly lonely about that.'

Cecil gave a vague shrug. 'It's what he preferred. Everyone finds comfort in different things.'

Edward certainly had been different. Brilliant but also

maddening. He'd been so precise, so relentlessly focused, that working with him could feel like trying to please a man who saw flaws in everything. Cecil had tolerated him for the sake of professionalism, but it had been an effort. Not that he could say any of that now—not to anyone, least of all his wife.

'Well, I know you didn't always get along,' Margaret said, cutting through his thoughts with typical bluntness, 'but it's still terribly sad. One moment you're working, and the next—sudden heart failure. Imagine that! It's such an awful thought.' She picked up her spoon and began sipping her soup. 'It could happen to any of us.'

Cecil did his best to suppress a sigh. 'It won't happen to any of us, Margaret. Edward's death was... unusual. These things are rare.'

'But how do you know that? Are you a doctor now?' she said lightly, dabbing her mouth with her serviette. 'He seemed perfectly fit and healthy. We both said so, didn't we?'

'Clearly, he wasn't as healthy as he appeared. He must have had a problem with his heart. That's all there is to it.' He set down his spoon with a quiet clink. 'If there's any comfort to be found, it's that he died doing what he loved —in his office, surrounded by his work.'

'Oh Cecil, that's hardly comforting,' Margaret said, shaking her head. 'He still had so many years ahead of him.'

'Maybe. But what's happened has happened, and we can't change that.'

Margaret finished her soup, folded her serviette with care, and rose from the table.

'Where are you off to?' he asked.

'My rehearsal, remember?' She stepped towards the

sideboard and checked her reflection in the mirror which hung above it.

'And a bowl of soup is enough for your dinner?'

'More than enough,' she said. 'You know I'm watching my waistline. The cook's made you that cream chicken you like. It's in the warming oven.' She leaned down and pressed a dry kiss to his cheek 'Don't wait up. We're running through the second act tonight, and it could go on for hours.'

'Very well,' said Cecil. 'Have a good evening, dear.'

She swept out with the click of heels on polished floorboards. Her perfume lingered faintly in the air.

Chapter Twelve

HALF AN HOUR LATER, Cecil knocked at the door of an apartment in an elegant building in Marylebone.

Vanessa answered the door barefoot and wrapped in a violet silk dressing gown. She had curling papers in her black hair.

'Cecil?' she said, eyebrows raised. 'What brings you here?'

'Margaret has a rehearsal,' he said, stepping inside. 'And I need to talk to you.'

'But I look a state!' She put her hands to her hair.

'You look beautiful.' He gave her a kiss.

'I need to put on a scarf.'

She scurried off to her bedroom while he stepped into the comfortable sitting room. A fire crackled in the hearth casting flickers across oil paintings and polished wood. Velvet armchairs were placed around a Persian rug and jazz music played on the gramophone.

Cecil sank into an armchair and loosened his tie. The weight always left his shoulders when he was in Vanessa's apartment.

Vanessa entered the room with a colourful scarf tied over her hair. She stepped over to the mahogany drinks cabinet and poured them both a whisky. Then she handed him a glass and perched on the arm of his chair.

'So?' she asked. 'What's all this about?'

'It's Edward Galloway,' he said. 'An old friend of his came to see me today—unexpectedly. And something about the whole thing felt off.'

'In what way?'

'Well, he brought his wife along. Dull creature. Didn't say much. But he was full of questions about Edward. It was all rather civil, but I couldn't shake the feeling that he was... prying.'

'Maybe he was,' she said lightly, taking a sip of her drink.

'But why?'

'His death was so sudden and everyone is questioning why.'

'He asked to see Edward's office. I let Miss Miller show him, I'd had enough by that point. The whole thing left a bad taste.'

Vanessa took her cigarette case from her dressing gown pocket, pulled out a cigarette and lit it. 'Darling, you're overthinking it,' she said, gently puffing out a cloud of smoke. 'Of course his friend wants to know more.'

Cecil didn't reply at first. He stared into his glass. 'I just... didn't like it,' he muttered. 'It felt like he was digging. And I can't help feeling that someone's going to find out.'

Vanessa pulled back slightly, her brow creased. 'Find out what, Cecil?'

'You know what,' he said quietly. 'I've felt it building for days now. A sort of pressure, like something's closing in. And when that man came to see me today—it was as if he could sense something.'

Vanessa studied him for a long moment. Then she reached out and gently pressed a fingertip to his lips. 'Shush,' she said. 'Don't work yourself into a state. There's nothing to find out. No one knows anything. The only person who was capable of working it out was Edward. And he's gone now, hasn't he?'

She smiled and put her cigarette to her lips.

Cecil tried to feel reassured but he couldn't shake the chill which had settled over him.

Chapter Thirteen

CURWEN FINE ARTS sat discreetly off Bloomsbury Square, its brass plaque understated, its tall windows veiled by ivory blinds.

'Here we are,' said Philip. 'It wasn't too difficult to find Vanessa Curwen was it? She's only around the corner from us.'

Augusta smiled. It had been a short walk. 'Let's find out how helpful she is,' she said.

Inside, the walls were papered in soft laurel green. Each painting was illuminated by a little brass picture lamp. A mahogany table stood in the far corner but no one sat in the plush velvet chairs which were arranged around it. Locked cases displayed miniatures and the air carried the scent of lavender.

'There's no one about,' Augusta whispered to Philip. 'Surely we could just walk out with one of these paintings.'

'May I help you?' Augusta startled as an attractive dark-haired lady stepped out from behind one of the partitions. Her hair was fashionably bobbed and wavy. She wore a long string of pearls and a stylish belted cardigan over a matching pleated skirt. Augusta had seen adverts of models in similar outfits in magazines.

'Miss Curwen?' ventured Philip.

She rested her feline gaze on him. 'Yes, that's right.'

'My name is Roger Parker. I was a friend of Edward Galloway. I hope you don't mind us calling on you like this, but I understand you knew him fairly well.'

A pause followed and Augusta noted the emotions which crossed Miss Curwen's face—first alarm, then a flash of irritation, before her features settled into a practised composure. The smile she offered was polite, but there was no warmth in it.

'Who told you that?' she asked.

'Someone at the National Gallery,' Philip replied. 'I forget who exactly.' He turned to Augusta. 'Can you remember, dear?'

Although she knew it was part of the act, Augusta resented the sudden pressure to improvise. 'I'm not sure,' she said with a vague smile. 'We've spoken to so many people.'

Miss Curwen's eyes moved between them, assessing. Her lips thinned.

'Well,' Philip continued, 'whoever it was, it hardly matters. I was just hoping to speak with someone who'd seen Edward recently. I regret to say I let our friendship lapse—life got busy, as it does. I meant to visit him, but somehow the months slipped by. Then I heard he'd died, and... well, it was quite a shock.'

Miss Curwen nodded and crossed to a painting on the wall, adjusting it by a fraction. It didn't need straightening, but she clearly felt the need to do something.

'It was a shock,' she said finally. 'But I'm afraid someone's misinformed you. I didn't know Edward Galloway particularly well. Our paths crossed because we were in the same field. I'm an art dealer, as you can see.' She gestured at the paintings around them. 'He and I met occasionally to discuss works which I thought would interest the gallery. We also saw one another at events—openings, lectures, and so on. But we weren't close. He always struck me as intelligent, courteous and deeply knowledgeable. I heard he was an artist himself, although I never saw any of his work.'

She finished with a poised smile.

'I see,' Philip said, shifting slightly. Augusta recognised the gesture as a sign of his mounting impatience. He wanted to push further, but he was bound by the role he was playing.

'He often worked late,' he said. 'I've been told that. Do you think he was the sort of man who allowed his work to consume him? Sometimes that kind of intensity can put a strain on a person—especially the heart.'

Miss Curwen shook her head. 'He was passionate, Mr Parker. Dedicated. But I hardly think his devotion to art contributed to his death. From what I heard, he enjoyed his work. I suspect, as others have said, that it was simply a tragic heart condition. An unfortunate event.'

'Well,' Philip said, 'thank you for your time. I must have been mistaken about your connection to him. But I appreciate you speaking with us. It's comforting to know he was well regarded.'

He made a small movement to leave, then paused.

'There's just one more thing, if you don't mind. His secretary mentioned that a painting appears to have gone missing from his office. Do you know anything about that?'

There was the smallest hesitation—barely a breath—then Miss Curwen recovered herself. Her voice was calm, but Augusta noticed a telltale flicker in her eyes.

'A missing painting?' she repeated. 'No, I know nothing about that. I couldn't tell you what paintings he had in his office. I last visited the gallery about three weeks ago. If something's gone missing, I suggest you speak with the staff. I really can't help you.'

The smile she gave them now was thinner.

'I believe the artist of the missing painting is popular at the moment, continued Philip. 'Veridiano. Apparently he's been rediscovered. Do you know much about him?'

Miss Curwen gave a little exasperated sigh but seemed willing to tell Philip more detail. 'Giovanni di Luca Veridiano,' she said. 'A Renaissance artist from Florence who is said to have died young around 1512. His existence was unknown to modern day art historians until some sketchbooks of his were found recently. To date, three paintings have been identified as works of his. *The Melancholy of Saint Aurelia*, *Allegory of the Four Humours* and *Portrait of a Widow with a Lark*.'

'The lark,' said Philip. 'Apparently that was the painting in Edward's office which has now gone missing. Miss Miller seemed concerned about it.'

'I see. Well if there was any cause for concern then the National Gallery would have raised the alarm by now.' She cocked her head to one side. 'Is that all? I'm quite busy.'

Augusta glanced around the empty gallery wondering what could be occupying Miss Curwen's time.

'That's all,' said Philip. 'Thank you for your time.'

Chapter Fourteen

'I THINK Vanessa Curwen knows something about the missing painting,' said Augusta as she and Philip made the short walk through the drizzle back to the shop and office. 'Her expression gave her away when you asked her about it.'

'I agree,' Philip said grimly. 'She recovered quickly, of course—but she knows more than she's letting on.' He exhaled sharply. 'It's maddening not being able to question these people more thoroughly. I have to pretend to be this well-meaning friend who hasn't seen Edward in years and I'm worried it's not terribly convincing. Someone is going to grow suspicious of us before long.'

'It's frustrating,' Augusta agreed. 'But we're getting somewhere. Every person we talk to adds another piece to the puzzle. Miss Curwen definitely knows more about that painting—and if we can prove she was at the National Gallery more recently than she claimed, then we'll know for certain she's lying.'

Philip nodded, his brow furrowed. 'If she said three weeks, and we find out it was more like three days…'

'Exactly,' said Augusta. 'I think we need to ask Miss Miller who's been coming and going.'

'Good idea.'

'And I think we need to speak to someone else too. Someone who knows a bit about the art world. Like you, Philip, I don't know much about art and it would be good to learn a little more about the fuss which the rediscovered artist has caused. Miss Curwen told us a little bit but I don't trust her.'

'Me neither. Who do you suggest we speak to?'

'I'll have a think.'

They stepped into the shop and found Lady Hereford in her bath chair by the counter talking to Fred. She gave them a broad grin when she saw them.

'There you are! I was just telling Fred here all about the Dowager Lady Pontypool.'

Augusta noticed Fred's expression seemed politely bored.

'Really?' said Augusta, taking off her coat and hanging it on its hook behind the counter. 'What has she been up to? She's only been at the hotel for about a week, hasn't she?'

'Exactly.' Lady Hereford pursed her lips in indignation. 'One week, Augusta. Seven days. And already she's stirring up trouble, just as I predicted. That's why I told you I might have to move out. I simply cannot bear it.'

'What's she done?' Augusta asked. She suspected it wouldn't be a matter of grave criminal behaviour.

'Held a very noisy tea party yesterday afternoon, that's what. And…' Lady Hereford's voice rose in disbelief, 'she didn't even invite me.'

'Presumably,' Augusta said delicately, 'you wouldn't have wanted to attend even if you had been invited?'

'Of course not,' Lady Hereford huffed. 'I would have

refused, naturally. But it's the principle of the thing. I occupy the suite next to hers. Simple manners dictate that she extend the courtesy of an invitation.'

Augusta bit the inside of her cheek to avoid smiling. The idea that Lady Hereford was affronted by not being invited to an event she had no desire to attend struck her as both amusing and entirely in character. 'I wouldn't let it trouble you,' she said. 'From what you've told me, she hardly sounds like someone worth sharing tea with.'

'And then there was the noise,' said the old lady. 'That was the true offence.'

'What made it so noisy?' asked Philip.

'For one thing, the Dowager Lady Pontypool has a dreadful laugh. Loud, shrill, and entirely false—a sort of honking bray that penetrates even the thickest walls. And the Russell Hotel does have quite thick walls.' Lady Hereford shook her head. 'She gathered some other loud-voiced guests who apparently found her long-winded anecdotes hilarious. They all laughed out of politeness, no doubt.'

'And you couldn't rest,' Augusta said.

'Precisely. I instructed Doris to put on my gramophone. Loudly.'

Augusta sighed. 'You tried to drown out the tea party with your gramophone?'

'Naturally. What other choice did I have? But can you believe the audacity, Augusta—the sheer, unrepentant nerve—when a bellboy knocked on my door not long after, informing me there had been a complaint about *my* noise?'

'Let me guess,' said Philip. 'The Dowager Lady Pontypool complained?'

'She did!' Lady Hereford's eyes widened dramatically. 'She had the gall to accuse me of disturbing the peace. I told the bellboy that if Lady Pontypool insisted on disturbing her neighbours, she ought not to be surprised if her neighbours made a little noise in return. The bellboy left rather quickly,' Lady Hereford added. 'He knew perfectly well who was in the right.'

Augusta could imagine the boy's discomfort. 'This sounds a bit like tit-for-tat,' she ventured.

'It is not tit-for-tat!' Lady Hereford snapped. 'It is the natural consequence of her unreasonable behaviour. And I've taken the sensible course of action—I have a meeting with the hotel manager later this afternoon to discuss the matter. The only satisfactory solution would be for the Dowager Lady Pontypool to vacate the premises entirely. That would restore peace and decorum to the Russell Hotel.'

'Have you spoken to her directly about the tea party?' Augusta asked.

'No. And I have no intention of doing so. I don't wish to stoop to petty squabbles. And, curiously, she hasn't mentioned the gramophone either. I suspect she knows she was in the wrong.'

Augusta suspected both ladies were being equally stubborn. 'I'm sorry you had such a trying afternoon yesterday,' she said. 'Let me make some tea—and I'm sure Sparky will cheer you up.'

'Oh, he always does.' Lady Hereford turned a fond smile towards the canary's cage. 'He has a remarkable ability to soothe frazzled nerves. Unlike certain dowagers I could mention.'

Sparky chirped obligingly as if to signal his agreement.

Chapter Fifteen

'WHAT DO YOU THINK?' asked Fred the following morning. He proudly showed Augusta the copy of *The Time Machine* by H.G. Wells which he'd been carefully repairing.

Augusta was impressed. 'It looks perfect, Fred!' She took the book from him and brushed her fingertips over the restored spine. The green cloth cover was clean and unblemished and she admired the embossed lettering gleaming on the cover. Fred's repairs were so subtle they would only be noticed by someone who knew what to look for.

'I think you've done a marvellous job,' Augusta said. 'And you've picked up the skill of book repairing in about a third of the time it took me.'

Fred gave a modest shrug, although his smile was proud. 'I have a good teacher, Augusta.'

'Oh yes, of course.' She grinned. 'That's the reason you've learned so quickly.' She handed the book back to him. 'It seems a shame to sell it now. If you want to keep it for yourself, I don't mind.'

'Oh no, we must put it out for sale,' said Fred. 'I don't

want to become too attached to my projects. And I like the idea of this book being enjoyed by someone again.'

Augusta hesitated for a moment. She wanted to tell Fred all about the investigation into Edward Galloway's death, it frustrated her that she had to keep it quiet. Fred had been helpful in previous investigations and she felt sure he could help with this one.

'You read a lot of periodicals, don't you Fred?' she asked.

'Yes. Well, my mother enjoys reading them so we have a lot lying about at home. I pick them up and read them too.'

'Any magazines about art?'

He thought for a moment. 'No, not art. My mother likes society magazines and fashion. And magazines about the home. Why do you ask?'

'Philip and I are working on a secret investigation,' said Augusta. 'I'm sorry I can't tell you more about it, Fred, but we've been sworn to secrecy. We need to know a little more about art and so I want to speak to someone who works on a publication about art.'

'I don't know many,' he replied. 'But *The Art Chronicle* is quite well-known. I've read it a few times in the library.'

'That sounds like a good place to start, thank you Fred. And as soon as I'm able to, I'll tell you what we're working on. I hate having to keep secrets.'

'Sometimes it's necessary, Augusta.' He smiled. As Augusta met his gaze she realised he probably knew now which case they were working on. He'd read about Edward Galloway's death in the newspaper and she imagined it wouldn't have taken him long to work it out.

. . .

That afternoon, Augusta and Philip made their way to the offices of *The Art Chronicle* on Fleet Street.

'What a busy place,' she remarked as they made their way along the crowded pavement. Everyone around them was in a hurry and a steady stream of motor cars and buses flowed past. Telegram and telephone cables were strung between the buildings high above their heads.

The walls of *The Art Chronicle* offices were covered in plum and gold wallpaper. Deep velvet armchairs sat beneath tasteful paintings and floral bouquets in large vases filled the air with the scent of lilies.

Mr Sandford, the magazine's editor, received them in his office. He wore a burgundy pinstriped suit, a large carnation in his lapel, and his grey hair—long at the collar—was swept back in wavy, theatrical style. A waxed moustache curled neatly at the corners of his upper lip.

'Mr Philip Fisher and Mrs Augusta Peel—we're private detectives,' said Philip as they entered his office. Augusta felt relieved they could be honest about their identities during this visit.

Mr Sandford raised an arched brow. 'Really? How terribly exciting. I don't often get to speak to detectives. What sort of art scandal are we talking about?'

Philip smiled faintly. 'Nothing dramatic, I'm afraid. A client has asked us to carry out some work for him connected to the art world. I'll admit it's a field we know little about, so we're hoping you might answer a few questions.'

'But of course,' said Sandford. 'Although first...' he reached over to a side table and plucked two copies of *The Art Chronicle* from a glossy stack. 'You simply must take these. Complimentary, of course. You'll have to purchase future editions.'

'Thank you,' said Philip, accepting the copies.

'You'll learn a lot from our publication,' Sandford continued, easing himself into a leather chair. 'It's educational and elegant. Auction news, gallery gossip, established geniuses and rising stars.'

A maid appeared with a tea tray and Sandford offered them both cigarettes, which they declined.

'So,' he said, crossing one leg over the other with flair, 'what would you like to know?'

'This client I mentioned,' said Philip, 'he's become quite enthusiastic about the recent discovery of a Renaissance artist.'

Sandford's expression brightened. 'Ah! Veridiano, isn't it?'

Philip blinked. 'Yes. I'm impressed.'

'Everyone's talking about him,' said the editor with glee. 'A most delicious story. Can you imagine? Forgotten for centuries! It all began when a collector of obscure antiquities stumbled across Veridiano's sketchbooks. They're real gems, by all accounts. And diaries too.' He inhaled on his cigarette, puckered his lips and blew out a ring of smoke.

'Where did the collector find the sketchbooks?' Augusta asked.

'They were in a box of paraphernalia which he bought at auction. You know the type of thing, don't you? A house gets cleared and all sorts of junk gets put into boxes which are then sold off by an auction house. Buyers rarely know what they're getting, but that's part of the fun, isn't it? They pay a small amount for something which has very little value and it raises some money for the estate to pay off death duties or what-have-you. Except in this case, the buyer found something extremely valuable indeed. Although you could argue, he made it valuable. He had the sense to know exactly what he'd found and he consulted the right people. Another buyer could have merely thrown the sketchbooks away and we'd all be none the wiser. And then there was a very odd coincidence.'

'And what was that?' asked Philip.

'A few months after the sketchbooks were found, a grand house in Hampstead was being cleared after the death of an elderly recluse. No one had any idea what treasures she had, but it turned out one of them was a Veridiano! It was believed to have been in the family of the recluse for generations, ever since some great-great-someone brought it back from Italy. Fascinating, isn't it? The painting is called *The Melancholy of Saint Aurelia* and the artist referred to it in his sketchbooks. It's a very striking painting of the saint. Subtle tears glisten on her cheeks as she cradles a snake. The serpent has created a great debate as experts try to decide what it symbolises within the context of the painting. It could be inner sin or it could be death. It could even represent knowledge or transformation.'

'Goodness,' said Philip. 'That sounds quite complicated.'

'It is. I can't claim to understand it all myself. At this publication, we merely report on these things. A specialist in Renaissance art at the National Gallery is doing a great deal of work on Veridiano.'

'Really?' said Philip. 'And who might that be?'

'Cecil White-Thomas. He's the Chief Conservator of Paintings at the gallery but he's taken a keen interest in the Renaissance his entire career. He's terribly excited about this new discovery. He even thinks Veridiano may have been part of a forgotten school.'

Chapter Sixteen

'A FORGOTTEN SCHOOL?' said Philip. 'How fascinating.'

Augusta hid a smile, amused by his attempt to sound interested in Renaissance art.

Mr Sandford re-crossed his legs and continued, 'Cecil White-Thomas has done a remarkable amount of research and discovered Giovanni di Luca Veridiano led a colourful life. He died young and his diaries suggest a disagreement with a powerful patron. Mr White-Thomas has uncovered a story that Veridiano was poisoned. There's also evidence his studio burned down shortly after his death.'

'Gosh,' said Augusta. 'How sad.'

'Indeed. It seems only a few of his works have survived and that could be a reason why he was forgotten. Now that we've learned something new, it means we need to look back at those times with a slightly different view. You could argue that this discovery has required a small rewriting of Renaissance art history.'

'It all sounds very interesting,' said Philip. 'So much so, that I rather wish I worked in the art world myself.'

Mr Sandford chuckled. 'I think your work as a private detective is equally interesting, Mr Fisher.'

'Do you know Cecil White-Thomas personally?' Augusta asked.

'I know him as an acquaintance,' said Mr Sandford, leaning back with a contented sigh. 'We've met at interviews, exhibitions, and other gatherings. He's tremendously knowledgeable. An absolute authority in his field.'

Philip nodded. 'And quite sadly, I heard another expert at the National Gallery passed away recently.'

'Oh yes,' Sandford said with a solemn note. 'Edward Galloway. A dreadful shock. So sudden, and completely unexpected. A great loss—he was highly respected.'

'Did you know him too?'

'In much the same way as Mr White-Thomas. We crossed paths now and again. We interviewed him for *The Art Chronicle* about a year ago and readers wrote in to tell me how much they enjoyed it. His secretary, Georgina Miller, used to work here. I was very sad when we lost her to the National Gallery. She's a lovely girl.' He inhaled on his cigarette and exhaled the smoke thoughtfully.

Philip shifted in his seat. 'As part of our research, we stopped by Vanessa Curwen's gallery the other day.'

A smile crept across Mr Sandford's face. 'Ah, yes. Miss Curwen. She's rather unforgettable, isn't she?'

'Yes,' Philip said neutrally. 'An expert in art, would you say?'

'Oh, certainly,' Sandford said. 'She has an excellent eye and a strong instinct for what sells. And, let's be honest, she also happens to be rather glamorous. When she enters a room, everyone notices—particularly in a crowd where most of the art world are ageing, grey-suited men who rarely look up from their catalogues.'

Augusta caught the faint note of amusement in Philip's glance.

'But don't let the fancy frocks fool you,' Sandford continued. 'She knows her business. She's made a great deal of money from it, and quite quickly too. She ensured *The Melancholy of Saint Aurelia* sold for a wonderful sum at auction.'

'She sold the painting?' asked Augusta, keen to clarify the art dealer had an interest in Veridiano.

'That's right. Oh she's very good at getting her hands on these deals. I wonder what I'm doing here, churning out articles when she's closing sales worth thousands.' He smiled. 'Still, my job has its perks. I get into every exhibition, every preview, and I meet some of the most interesting minds in the field. I like to think I have a decent breadth of knowledge, but I never had the patience to become a proper academic. Hence, editor.' He gave a self-deprecating shrug. 'I suppose it's a comfortable place to land.'

'What about *Portrait of a Widow with a Lark*,' asked Philip. 'Do you know much about that one?'

'That was found in a vestry in a Croydon church,' said Sandford with a chuckle. 'Astonishing isn't it? We think it must have hung in the vestry for centuries but it had been taken down from the wall and was stored behind the wardrobe when it was found. Mr Cecil-White is having a look at it as we speak.'

Augusta and Philip exchanged a glance, silently agreeing they wouldn't mention it was now missing from Galloway's office.

Augusta thought while she took a sip of tea. 'The collector who found the sketchbooks,' she said. 'Who was he?'

'Some old fellow who has a shop of curios just off Tottenham Court Road,' replied Sandford.

'Do you know his name?'

'Ridley I think it is. His shop's mostly filled with cheap junk but now and again he has something valuable in there. And that Veridiano sketchbook was quite a find!'

Chapter Seventeen

Vanessa Curwen sipped her cocktail slowly, enjoying the sensation of the chilled glass on her fingertips. She placed down her drink, drew out her silver cigarette case, flicked it open, and placed a cigarette between her lips. Before she could reach for her lighter, a man at the bar beside her leaned in and lit it for her.

'Thank you,' she said coolly, not even glancing his way.

'Do you come here often?' he ventured.

He was clearly planning to be a nuisance. She gave him a contemptuous look and turned her gaze to the shiny black staircase which descended into the bar from street level.

As if on cue, Cecil appeared at the top of the stairs. He descended the steps two at a time, his hat in his hand. His eyes met hers and he crossed the floor with purpose, his jaw set.

'Must we meet in this awful place?' he muttered as he reached her. 'You know I hate this bar.'

'Don't be grumpy, Cecil.' She gripped the collar of his coat and pulled him in for a kiss. The man who'd lit her cigarette sidled away. 'This is one of my favourite places,' she added.

'I don't see why.' He pulled away and glanced around. 'And this had better be important. Margaret and I are entertaining tonight. I had to concoct an elaborate excuse about being called urgently to the gallery. She'll interrogate me the moment I get back.'

'I'm sure you'll manage,' said Vanessa. 'You always do.' She gestured to the barman. 'He'll have a scotch. Neat.'

Cecil scowled. 'I haven't got time for a drink.'

'Oh, come now. If you're needed at the gallery for an hour or two, surely you can spare five minutes with me?' She looked up at him through her eyelashes. 'Anyway, who are you entertaining tonight?'

'Sir Charles and his wife.'

She smiled. 'How frightfully proper.'

The barman set a glass before him. Cecil picked it up and took a gulp. 'All right,' he said tersely. 'What's this about?'

'I thought you'd want to know that Roger Parker—the old friend of Edward Galloway—called on me yesterday. He brought his wife along with him—a quiet, mousy thing.'

Cecil stiffened. 'And what did he ask you?'

'Well it was all rather strange. He began by telling me he felt guilty about not having seen Galloway recently. Then he claimed someone at the gallery told him we'd been friends.'

'Who?'

'He said they couldn't remember who.'

'That's a bit strange,' said Cecil, scratching his neck. 'And what did you say?'

'I told them the truth—that Galloway and I weren't close. That we crossed paths professionally, nothing more.

Then Parker asked whether I thought Galloway overworked himself, no doubt wondering if that's what brought on the heart attack.' She took a drag on her cigarette. 'And after that he asked me about the painting.'

'What painting?'

'Which one do you think? The Veridiano which was in Galloway's office. Apparently Miss Miller told them it had gone missing.'

Cecil sighed and rubbed his brow. 'Why would she mention that to them?' he said. 'It's no concern of theirs.'

'It seems Mr and Mrs Parker have made it their concern. I've no idea why.'

'So what did you say?'

'I told them I felt sure there was nothing to worry about.'

'And did that work?'

She shrugged. 'I think so. But it's strange they were told I was close to Galloway. Who would have told them that and why? I don't understand why this Roger Parker is going about speaking to people. Why not just turn up at the funeral and leave it at that? Why come to my gallery specifically? There's something funny about it.'

'You're right, Vanessa. It's funny indeed. He seems harmless enough. And his wife—well, she's clearly no one to worry about. But yes... I don't see why they're digging like this. Going from person to person. Perhaps we shouldn't concern ourselves too much. At the end of the day, does it really matter?'

'No, perhaps not,' she said. 'But I thought you should know, since they've already been to see you. And Miss Miller too, apparently. Who knows who else they'll call on next?'

Cecil finished off his drink and set the glass back on the bar.

'Will you stay for another?' she asked.

'I'd love to,' he said. 'But I can't. Not tonight. And while I appreciate you thought this was urgent, I think, in hindsight, it could have waited. Don't you?'

She turned away, concealing her hurt expression. Perhaps it could have waited. But she enjoyed knowing she'd forced Cecil to spin yet another lie to his wife. She didn't care if Margaret found out about their affair. In fact, part of her hoped she would. But Cecil? Cecil was very worried about Margaret discovering his secret.

'Very well,' she said coldly. 'You go back to your wife. I'll amuse myself. Perhaps I'll chat to the charming gentleman who lit my cigarette.'

Cecil paused. 'That's your idea of revenge, is it?'

She gave him a slow, deliberate smile and fluttered her lashes. 'What's a lady to do when she's left all alone?'

'I don't have time for your games tonight, Vanessa,' he snapped. 'I really do have to get back to dinner.'

He turned and strode toward the stairs, his hat already on his head. Vanessa watched him go, the bitterness rising like bile. She hated it when he dismissed her. She hated the way he brushed her off when it suited him. And tonight, he'd done just that.

He should have known better.

Chapter Eighteen

'Hello again, Mr and Mrs Parker,' said Georgina Miller, her expression warm but wary. 'Is there something else I can help you with?' The secretary got to her feet and stood politely by her desk.

Three other women shared the office with Miss Miller. All worked at their typewriters while casting fleeting glances at Augusta and Philip.

'We were wondering if you had any luck finding the Veridiano painting which went missing from Edward's office,' said Philip. 'The *Portrait of a Widow with a Lark*.'

'Oh yes!' Her face brightened. 'I found some paperwork in his office. He'd arranged for the painting to be sent to a gallery in Florence.'

'Oh,' said Philip. 'Is that a normal thing to happen?'

'Quite normal. The National Gallery often loans paintings to other galleries.'

'Paintings which the gallery owns, presumably. Did the gallery actually own *Portrait of a Widow with a Lark*? I heard the picture was found only recently in a church in Croydon.'

'I don't know about all that, I'm sorry.' She bit her lip, as if anxious that she couldn't fully answer the question.

The sudden loan of the painting to an Italian gallery seemed odd to Augusta. As Philip had mentioned, it had only recently been found.

'Well I suppose it's good news you've found what's happened to the painting,' said Philip. 'Its sudden disappearance didn't sit well with me. I was worried someone might have taken advantage of Edward's death. We'd hate for that to happen, wouldn't we?'

Miss Miller nodded. 'Of course. We all would.'

Philip lowered his voice a little. 'I hope you don't mind me asking, but do you know Miss Curwen?'

'You mean Vanessa Curwen, the art dealer? I know who she is.'

'Does she visit the gallery often?'

'Quite often.'

'Can you recall when you last saw her here?'

Miss Miller tilted her head, thinking. 'It wasn't long ago, perhaps a week ago. She called on Mr Galloway. I made coffee for them both.'

Augusta felt the familiar surge of satisfaction that came when a suspicion was confirmed.

'That's interesting,' said Philip smoothly. 'Can you remember the day, by any chance?'

Miss Miller frowned. 'Not exactly. But I think it might have been Thursday. Yes—Thursday sounds right.'

'Thank you,' Philip said. 'You've been very helpful. We're just trying to make sense of everything. It's been a rather strange time trying to piece together the final days of an old friend. I'm sorry for troubling you again. We'll leave you in peace.'

'Before you go,' she said, 'there's someone in Mr Galloway's office you might remember.'

Augusta's stomach knotted. She'd been worried this might happen. Someone who'd been close to Galloway who might expect recognition. The danger of their cover slipping loomed suddenly large.

'Oh really?' said Philip, keeping his voice light. 'Who's that?'

'Mr Galloway's daughter, Lillian. She wanted to spend some time in his office. I expect you'll want to see her.'

Augusta glanced at Philip and, for a brief second, his eyes conveyed the concern she also felt.

'That's wonderful,' said Philip to Miss Miller. 'Of course we'd like to see dear Lillian.'

Chapter Nineteen

AUGUSTA'S BREATH quickened as she and Philip followed Miss Miller to Mr Galloway's office. Would his daughter realise they hadn't been friends of her father? Would she say something which risked their cover being broken?

Inside the office a young woman sat quietly at the desk. She turned her head in their direction when they entered the room but didn't get to her feet.

Augusta was struck by Miss Galloway's resemblance to her father. She had the same dark hair and grey piercing eyes. Her clothes were unconventional—a colourful scarf, a baggy tweed jacket worn over a loose silk blouse and gentlemen's-cut trousers. Her lace-up leather shoes were battered and a scruffy leather satchel lay on the desk in front of her.

'This is Mr and Mrs Parker,' said Miss Miller. 'Mr Parker was a good friend of your father's. Have you met before?'

Lillian Galloway stared at them with no hint of recognition.

'No, we haven't,' said Philip. 'Edward mentioned you

many times, Miss Galloway, but we never had the pleasure of meeting, did we?'

The young woman shook her head.

Miss Miller glanced at them all and said, 'Well, I suppose I'd better get back to my work.'

'I'm very sorry about the death of your father,' said Augusta once Miss Miller had left the room. 'Please accept our condolences.'

Miss Galloway had turned away now and was surveying the room. 'I just wanted to see his office.'

'Have you been here before?' asked Augusta.

'No. I never called on him here.' She folded her arms and turned back to them. 'How did you know my father? I don't recall him mentioning you.'

Philip cleared his throat, giving himself time to think. 'We worked together in Canada during the war,' he said.

'But you're not Canadian.'

'No, I'm not. I'm British. And your father wasn't Canadian either. It was a project we were working on there.'

She said nothing and turned away again.

'Do you live in London?' Augusta asked her.

She nodded. 'Yes. I'm a poet.'

'Is that so?' said Augusta, interested. 'What sort of poetry do you write?'

Miss Galloway blew out a sigh. There was something sulky about her manner. Augusta wondered if she was always like this or if her mood was a response to her father's death. 'What sort of poetry?' Miss Galloway repeated. 'The sort that makes respectable people shift in their chairs. I'm told it's modern, but sometimes people say that when they dislike something but can't quite explain why. I write about things no one wants to remember. Absences. The way people quietly vanish… into war, into grief, into silence. I'm not interested in roses or romance.

My verses don't flatter anyone. And… my poems don't sell. Which I'm told is a sign of their artistic merit.'

Philip gave Augusta a puzzled glance and she suppressed a smile.

'Have you had any poems published?' she asked Miss Galloway.

'I've had a few published in poetry magazines. I'm trying to find an agent, but it's difficult finding someone who actually understands what I write.'

'Did your father enjoy your poetry?' Augusta asked.

The young woman gave a derisive sniff. 'He never read any of it. And I wouldn't have wanted him to.'

'When did you last see him?'

'When did I last see him? Oh ages ago. About a year ago.' She picked up the satchel from the desk and got to her feet. She was tall and lean, just as her father had been.

'A year?' said Augusta.

Miss Galloway nodded and made her way to the door. 'We weren't close,' she added before leaving the room.

Chapter Twenty

Philip raised his eyebrows as Lillian Galloway left the room and quietly closed the door behind her.

'What did you make of young Miss Galloway?' he whispered to Augusta.

'Odd,' Augusta replied. 'But perhaps I'm being unfair. Her father has just died.'

'By her own admission, she wasn't close to him. But that's not to say she isn't grieving in her own way.'

'Absolutely. And a difficult relationship can make the grief more complicated,' said Augusta. 'If you haven't seen your father in over a year then receive the news he's suddenly died…' She tailed off, reminded of her estrangement from her own parents. 'Well it can be difficult. I imagine guilt must play a part too. The guilt that you didn't make amends before they died.'

Philip nodded. 'She seems… angry.'

'Yes she does. In fact, she reminds me a little of myself at her age. When my parents tried to force me into a marriage I didn't want, I packed a bag and ran away to London.' She shook her head gently at the memory. 'I was certainly angry then—furious at the world.'

'Did you write any poetry?' Philip asked with a wry smile.

'No. And don't be mean about Miss Galloway's poetry. I realise it's not the sort of thing you enjoy but she might be quite good at it. She's had some poems printed in magazines which suggests some talent. I'd like to read them. They might give us some insight into what's going on in her mind.'

'True,' agreed Philip. 'And I'd like to understand more about her relationship with her father. There was clearly tension between them.'

'But once again we're hampered by our undercover role,' said Augusta. 'Roger Parker has no reason to question Miss Galloway about her father. Nor does his wife.'

Philip sighed. 'It's becoming more and more limiting, but we'll keep working on it. Wasn't it interesting to hear from Miss Miller that Miss Curwen called on Galloway recently? Curwen told us she'd last visited the gallery three weeks ago. Now we know it was a lie.'

'Just as we suspected,' said Augusta. 'Do you think Miss Curwen had an interest in *Portrait of a Widow with a Lark*? We've learned she sold *The Melancholy of Saint Aurelia* for a good sum of money. I'm sure she would have liked to have done the same with the painting of the widow.'

'She must have been interested in it,' said Philip. 'And she must be rather disappointed that it's currently on its way to Italy... Now that reminds me.' He held up a finger. 'Let's see if we can find the paperwork Miss Miller mentioned confirming *Portrait of a Widow with a Lark* is being loaned to a gallery in Florence.' He stepped over to the desk, opened a drawer and put on his reading glasses.

Augusta felt a stab of concern. 'We don't want to get

caught looking through his things. Miss Miller could return at any moment.'

'Then let's be quick,' said Philip. 'Help me.'

Augusta stepped over to the desk, listening out for footsteps on the other side of the door. She pulled out a drawer and quickly rummaged through its contents. Pens, paper clips, notebooks and folded pieces of paper which she had to unfold and look at. It was difficult to keep her mind on the task with the nagging unease they could be caught at any moment.

Philip pulled out another drawer with a noisy scrape.

'Shush!' urged Augusta, her heart pounding. 'Someone will hear!'

'You're whispering louder than the noise the drawer made,' he retorted.

'I'm not, I'm—' Then she heard the sound of footsteps in the corridor outside. She pushed in the drawer, Philip did the same, and they both made their way over to the door.

They were just about to open it when it was opened from the other side.

'Hello,' said Miss Miller. She peered past them. 'Has Miss Galloway left?'

'Yes. Just now,' said Philip. 'And we're heading off too. It was nice to speak to her.'

'Good.' Miss Miller smiled. 'Well I'd better lock up the office again.'

'Absolutely,' said Augusta. 'We're just leaving.'

Miss Miller bid them farewell but her gaze lingered on them as if she were considering something.

Was it possible she was growing suspicious of them?

Chapter Twenty-One

LILLIAN GALLOWAY TIGHTENED her scarf and leaned into the cold northern wind which blew down Charing Cross Road.

Mr and Mrs Parker had lied to her.

Just like her father had.

Roger Parker had claimed he and her father had worked together in Canada during the war. But that was impossible. She knew her father's war record. He had never set foot in Canada.

So why lie?

Why had the deceit followed her father's death like a shadow?

She paused at the window of a bookshop and peered in at the display. But she paid little attention to the books themselves, her thoughts were elsewhere.

She wasn't mourning. Not really. Her father had left her long ago—not with death, but with indifference. For years, he had buried himself in his work with the fervour of a man hiding from something.

From her.

From his wife.

From the past he never spoke of.

She turned away from the window, feeling the chill from the wind. Then she tied her scarf tighter still and continued walking.

Chapter Twenty-Two

'Let's stop here,' said Philip. 'And I'll show you what I found in Galloway's office.' He stepped into a sheltered doorway in a side street next to the National Gallery, put on his reading glasses and pulled a crumpled piece of paper from his pocket.

Augusta was impressed. 'You found something useful?'

'I think so.'

She joined him in the doorway and peered closely at the paper as he smoothed it out.

'It's a letter from the Galleria Fiorentina delle Belle Arti,' said Philip. 'It must be the gallery in Florence which Georgina Miller told us about. It says, "We are pleased to confirm that your esteemed painting titled *Portrait of a Widow with a Lark*, oil on canvas, attributed to Giovanni di Luca Veridiano, has been formally accepted for temporary loan to the Galleria Fiorentina delle Belle Arti, as part of our upcoming exhibition *Volti Nascosti del Rinascimento*, commencing 14th November 1922."'

'So Galloway must have arranged the loan,' said

Augusta. 'Presumably with the agreement of the church in Croydon it was found in.'

'Yes I presume so,' said Philip. 'And despite his death, the loan has gone ahead. Someone went into his office, took the painting, packaged it up and sent it off.'

'And managed to do it without Galloway's secretary, Miss Miller, being aware of it,' said Augusta. 'That still strikes me as odd.'

'Yes it is.' Philip shrugged. 'But we have paperwork confirming it.' He folded up the letter and pushed it back into his pocket. 'Shall we go and see Mr Ridley now? The curios seller who found Veridiano's long-lost sketchbooks.'

'Good idea.'

The cold wind pulled at Augusta's hat and coat as she and Philip made their way north up Charing Cross Road and Tottenham Court Road. By the time they reached Mr Ridley's strange little shop, Augusta felt tired from the effort of battling the strong breeze.

The shop had a grimy bow window and crooked steps leading up to a paint-peeled door. The name "Ridley's Antiquaries and Curios" was written in faded gold lettering above.

Inside, the shop was dim, lit only by shaded lamps and the weak grey light filtering in through the front window. The air smelled of musty old paper and tobacco.

A dusty cabinet near the door held sepia-toned photographs of stiffly posed people, their names long lost to time. Beside them lay a delicate mourning brooch and a warped wooden snuff box. Nearby, a recipe book lay open to a page for seed cake, its pages mottled with grease. On the shelves, Augusta spotted a barometer shaped like a ship's wheel, a china doll's head and a tiny glass bottle, clouded with age, and labelled Elixir of Lavender.

Augusta recalled the editor of *The Art Chronicle* describing the shop as being filled with cheap junk. His words had been remarkably accurate. Some shelves of old books caught her eye, however, and she felt an urge to have a good look through them.

Everything was silent apart from the heavy tick of a clock. Augusta glanced around, wondering where Mr Ridley could be. Philip caught her gaze and gave her a bemused look. He was clearly wondering the same thing.

They eventually found him sitting in a chair at the back of the shop examining pieces of what appeared to be a brass telescope. He was a small, round man with wisps of grey hair around his ears and a pair of pince-nez perched on the end of his nose.

'Hello,' said Philip.

'How can I help?' replied Ridley, without looking up. He wore a moth-eaten cardigan over a tweed waistcoat and knitted fingerless gloves.

'Mr Ridley?' said Philip. 'My name's Roger Parker. I was a friend of Edward Galloway. This is my wife, Amelia Parker.'

Ridley blinked slowly, removed his pince nez and gave them a sleepy look. 'Galloway,' he repeated. 'Yes, a sad loss.'

'I hope you don't mind the intrusion,' said Philip, glancing around. 'We were hoping for a few minutes of your time.'

'You'll have to be quick. I close soon for lunch.'

'We're speaking to people who knew Edward,' said Augusta, 'to get a better sense of his final few months. The news of his death came as quite a shock.'

Ridley gave a short nod. 'Yes. It was sudden.'

'Did you know him well?' Philip asked.

He shrugged. 'No, not well. But he had a good eye, and unlike many in his profession, he had integrity. A rare thing these days.'

'Did you see him recently?' Augusta asked.

'Three or four weeks ago, I'd say. He liked to visit and see what had come in recently. Especially since I found some valuable old sketchbooks... there's been a lot of interest in my shop since then.'

'The Veridiano sketchbooks?' asked Augusta.

'Yes, that's right.' The mention of them enlivened him a little and he put down his pieces of telescope on a little side table. 'They were one of those discoveries I've always dreamed of.'

'How did you come by them?'

'They were tucked away in a rather unpromising box I picked up at auction. A miscellaneous lot. And just once in a while, there's treasure hidden within. This box didn't look like much. Some ledgers, a bundle of letters, a cracked inkpot, and a few tattered sketchbooks by someone who, frankly, had no talent whatsoever. But then I spotted a pair of small, leather-bound volumes tied together with string. Faded parchment, worn edges... and when I opened the first one, I nearly dropped it.'

Philip raised an eyebrow. 'Why?'

'The date. The entries were over four hundred years old! It set my heart racing. The ink was faded but legible in places. The writing was Italian and it was accompanied by some wonderfully expressive sketches. Whoever the writer was, he had an artist's hand and a keen eye for observation. I don't speak much Italian myself, but I knew immediately that I was looking at something special. So I took them to a chap I know at the National Gallery who has a particular interest in the Renaissance.

Cecil White-Thomas. He was quite astonished by them!' He gave a proud chuckle. 'He carried out a remarkable amount of research and eventually it became clear the diaries belonged to a painter called Giovanni di Luca Veridiano. A name which had previously been lost to history.'

'A lost genius,' said Philip.

'Absolutely! Three paintings of his have now turned up. Discoveries like this are never the work of one man. They're a chain of small accidents and timely choices. I just happened to open the right box on the right day.'

He paused for a moment, his gaze drifting back to the pieces of telescope. 'Galloway was very interested in Veridiano, just like the rest of us.'

'I heard he was working on Veridiano's *Portrait of a Widow with a Lark* at the time of his death,' said Philip.

'Yes, he was very fond of that painting.'

'He arranged for it to be loaned to a gallery in Florence. It's on its way there now.'

A pause followed. Ridley pulled a puzzled expression. 'Really?'

'Yes. Edward's secretary, Miss Miller, found the paperwork.'

Ridley scratched his head. 'A gallery in Florence? Which one?'

'The Galleria Fiorentina delle Belle Arti,' said Augusta.

'And the painting's on its way there? No… that doesn't make sense to me. *Portrait of a Widow with a Lark* had only just been found. Galloway and White-Thomas were overjoyed about it, I'm certain neither of them would have wanted to let it out of their sight. To allow that painting to leave our shores? No. I don't think they would do that.'

Philip glanced at Augusta and raised an eyebrow. Ridley was echoing their own surprise about the loan.

'Do you think there's something suspicious about it?' Philip asked him.

'Suspicious?' He thought for a moment. 'No, I don't think there can be anything suspicious about it. If Miss Miller has the paperwork for it all then I don't suppose we can question it. It's just surprising.' He sighed. 'Perhaps Galloway wasn't thinking straight before his death. Maybe his heart problems had caused his health to suffer and his mind was affected...' He gave a shrug. 'That's the only explanation I can think of.'

Chapter Twenty-Three

'WELL I'M pleased Mr Ridley was surprised *Portrait of a Widow with a Lark* has been loaned to the gallery in Florence,' said Augusta once she and Philip had left his shop. 'We thought it was odd, didn't we?'

Philip nodded. 'We need to speak to Mr White-Thomas again. I'd like to see what he makes of it all.'

Cecil White-Thomas kept them waiting when they returned to the National Gallery. When he eventually admitted them to his office, he was courteous but Augusta detected a slight frost beneath the politeness as they took their seats.

'We're sorry to trouble you again,' said Philip. 'I have one or two questions about Edward but first I must say I've only just learned about your remarkable work uncovering the legacy of the Renaissance artist Giovanni di Luca Veridiano.'

The iciness in White-Thomas's manner melted a little, he was clearly a man who enjoyed compliments.

'Ah yes. That discovery has consumed much of my time over the past year. Quite a revelation, really. It took a while to piece it all together, but the more I investigated, the clearer it became—Veridiano was a significant talent in the early Renaissance.'

He sat back a little, clearly enjoying the opportunity to explain more. 'He died young. In mysterious circumstances. There was a fire at his studio in Florence—officially accidental, but I believe otherwise. He'd fallen out with a powerful patron, and from what I've uncovered, there are hints the fire was set deliberately. A silencing, if you will. Many of his works were destroyed, and his name all but erased.'

His hands came together, fingertips pressed in a steeple. 'But now, slowly, his work is being recovered. As more experts recognise his style, more paintings have come to light. It's an extraordinary time for art historians. Quite enthralling.'

Augusta noted the enthusiastic gleam in his eyes. 'It must be deeply rewarding,' she said, 'to spend your life in a field and then uncover a forgotten master.'

'Oh yes,' White-Thomas said proudly. 'An opportunity which comes but once in a lifetime. I really am extremely privileged to have been involved. I don't take it for granted you know. It could so easily have been another expert in another generation. So it really has been down to pure luck. In fact, it doesn't feel as though I found Veridiano at all. It seems like he found me.' He gave a supercilious smile which Augusta found pompous.

'Incredible,' said Philip, pretending to flatter him some more. 'After all this excitement, you must have been quite surprised when Edward arranged for *Portrait of a Widow with a Lark* to be loaned to the Galleria Fiorentina delle Belle Arti in Italy.'

White-Thomas's eyebrows lifted, as if he was surprised they'd learned about this. Augusta sensed he wished to ask them how they knew, but instead he adopted a nonchalant manner. 'I'm afraid your late friend Edward was rather like that. Impulsive and unpredictable at times. I disagreed with the arrangement of course, but he was adamant he wished the painting to be part of an exhibition the gallery is holding. It is, after all, in Florence. The town which Veridiano lived and worked in. *Volti Nascosti del Rinascimento* I believe the exhibition is called. *Hidden Faces of the Renaissance*. In fact, I plan to visit it myself.'

'Edward arranged for the painting to be sent to Florence but his secretary, Miss Miller, knew nothing about it,' said Philip. 'Do you think that's odd?'

White-Thomas laughed. 'Of course it's odd. But that was Edward for you. You recall what he was like, don't you? He was a law unto himself.'

'I expect you're keen for the painting to return here,' said Philip. 'I heard you and Edward were both doing a great deal of work on it.'

'Yes. Although I had finished my part. I'm more interested in collating the information on all three works which have been uncovered to date. I've begun work on compiling a Catalogue Raisonné of Veridiano's works.' He patted a pile of papers on his desk. 'It's only a short list so far, but I feel confident more will be found. It's important word gets out about his work and then we might find more forgotten paintings of his which have been hanging in drawing rooms, council chambers, hotels... who knows? Not just here but abroad too. There must be works of his in Italy. I fear I shall have to spend quite a bit of time there soon to look for them.'

'I wish you all the best in doing so,' said Philip. 'Thank you for speaking to us again.'

They readied themselves to leave and White-Thomas showed them to the door.

'There's just something which remains puzzling,' Philip said to him. 'Why didn't Edward's death delay the transportation of the painting?'

White-Thomas scowled, his hand on the handle of the door. 'Why should it have?'

'The painting was removed from Edward's office the morning after he died,' said Philip. 'And its removal was so sudden that Miss Miller was surprised by it too. She didn't see who'd moved it. And his office is kept locked. Surely the people who arrived to collect the painting would have needed to ask Miss Miller for the key?'

White-Thomas pulled open the door. 'She obviously wasn't around at the time so they asked someone else. The security guards have keys too.'

Philip paused, giving this some thought. Augusta noticed White-Thomas's jaw clench with frustration.

'Can you be really sure the painting is on its way to Florence?' Philip asked him. 'Perhaps someone took it?'

The pale hooded eyes behind White-Thomas's spectacles grew colder now. 'Look,' he said finally, breaking the stillness, 'please don't take this the wrong way, Mr Parker... but I'm struggling to understand why you're taking such an interest. I appreciate the discovery of a lost Renaissance artist has stirred up a lot of excitement, but the details of your late friend's work and what became of the paintings he was handling are really no concern of yours.'

'Oh, quite right,' said Philip lightly. 'I'm just the sort of fellow who gets caught up in the details. Miss Miller seemed surprised when she saw the painting had gone. It made me wonder if something more had happened. That perhaps, in the confusion after my friend's death, someone had... taken advantage.'

'But that's clearly not the case,' White-Thomas said sharply.

'No, of course not,' said Philip. 'It's good to have it cleared up.'

'Indeed. Now, I'm rather busy. If you have further questions, I suggest you speak to Miss Miller. She'll be far more informed about Mr Galloway's affairs.'

Chapter Twenty-Four

'I DON'T THINK Cecil White-Thomas is going to be particularly cooperative with us from now on,' said Augusta once they'd left his office. 'He clearly didn't like us asking about the painting. Did you notice how tense he became?'

'I noticed,' said Philip. 'He seemed particularly irritable, didn't he? I wonder if he knows more than he's admitting.'

'I think he does,' said Augusta. 'For someone who rediscovered Veridiano, he seems to have had surprisingly little involvement with the loan of the painting to the gallery in Florence. He'd been studying the artist for months. Surely he'd want to oversee what happened to the painting?'

'I agree. And what's to say someone hasn't stolen it? Both White-Thomas and Miss Miller seem happy to accept it was removed from Galloway's office and is currently on its way to Florence. But we haven't come across anyone yet who saw it being moved, have we?'

'I've just had a thought,' said Augusta, lowering her

voice as they walked through a gallery of Dutch masters. 'We could send a telegram to the gallery and ask them to let us know once *Portrait of a Widow with a Lark* has arrived.'

'Good idea,' said Philip. 'And if it arrives there safely, then we know it hasn't been stolen. And if it doesn't turn up there?'

'Then it has been stolen.'

Philip dropped his voice to a whisper, 'And Galloway's death could be connected?'

'It must be. Someone must have poisoned him to get their hands on that painting.'

They left the gallery and paused at the edge of Trafalgar Square. Pigeons scattered across the flagstones in a flurry of wings, and low grey clouds billowed over the statue of Admiral Nelson high up on his column.

Philip pulled the letter from the Florence gallery from his pocket. 'There's no address on this,' he said. 'That's strange.'

'We can find the address in a travel book,' said Augusta. 'Baedeker's Guide to Italy will list it.'

Philip grinned. 'Of course. We can get a copy from one of the bookshops on Charing Cross Road.'

A short while later, they sat in a nearby tearoom and Augusta leafed through a copy of Baedeker's *Guide to Northern Italy*. She found the pages for Florence and searched through the listings for the Galleria Fiorentina delle Belle Arti.

Then she read through them again.

'I can't see it,' she said.

'Shall I have a look?' asked Philip, putting down his tea cup and pulling out his reading glasses.

Augusta handed him the book.

'You're right,' he said a few moments later. 'It's not listed, is it?'

Augusta felt puzzled. 'I'll have a look at the map at the back.' She took the book back from him and pulled out the city map for Florence tucked into the endpapers. She opened it out on the table, careful to keep it away from a small spill of milk.

'Looking at this map makes me want to travel again,' she said wistfully. 'I haven't been abroad since the end of the war.'

Philip nodded. 'Neither have I, now I think about it. I suppose after everything, we both just wanted a sense of home again. Still... perhaps next spring? A trip to Italy? Before the heat sets in?'

She met his gaze and the thought of the trip made her heart flutter. 'I'd like that,' she grinned. 'I'd like that a lot.'

But then a thought of Philip's wife came to mind. The pair were estranged but they weren't divorced. Augusta couldn't entertain the idea of travelling to Italy with a married man.

Her heart sank again at the thought. She returned her gaze to the guidebook. 'But for now, we're not planning a holiday, we're trying to find a gallery.'

She looked at the key on the map. The names of the museums and galleries were listed in neat, efficient type and each was accompanied by a numbered reference to the city map. The Uffizi, the Pitti Palace, the Bargello, the Accademia... but no Galleria Fiorentina delle Belle Arti.

'Nothing here,' she said after a moment. 'If it exists, it must be very small. Or perhaps it's not the sort of gallery which welcomes tourists, maybe it's just for people in the art world.'

Philip pulled out the letter again. 'The exhibition is *Volti Nascosti del Rinascimento. Hidden Faces of the Renaissance* I think White-Thomas said. That sounds to me like the sort of exhibition which would be open to the public.' He scratched his chin as he thought. 'Maybe the gallery is simply too small to be included.'

Augusta frowned, unconvinced. 'But Florence isn't a sprawling metropolis. If it were a proper gallery, however modest, you'd think it would want the publicity. Why go to the trouble of running it if nobody knows it exists?'

Philip gave a thoughtful nod. 'Perhaps the guide's out of date. It could be a new gallery, opened after publication.'

'Possibly. Although I think these guides are updated every year.' Augusta sat back in her chair and sighed. 'The more we look into this, the stranger it gets. The painting vanished from Mr Galloway's office almost immediately after his death. No one knows who removed it and Miss Miller didn't even realise it was gone. And now, when we try to find this gallery—it's nowhere to be found.'

Philip hesitated. 'That doesn't mean it doesn't exist.'

'No,' she said, 'but it's suspicious. There are too many odd little pieces, Philip. Nothing quite fits.'

'The gallery must exist,' said Philip. 'White-Thomas said he would probably go to the exhibition.'

'True.' Augusta considered this. 'But are we sure we believe him?'

'Well... that's a good point. I don't know. But let's take him at his word for now. If the painting has been stolen then Cecil-White will soon realise when he sees it's missing from the exhibition. And perhaps before then...' he added. 'If it doesn't arrive at the gallery in Florence then they'll no doubt contact the National Gallery and ask them where it is.'

Augusta took a sip of tea as she thought. 'Perhaps we've become too fixated by the painting. Perhaps it has nothing to do with Edward Galloway's murder. And by concentrating so much on its whereabouts, perhaps we're missing something else entirely?'

'Well that's a very good point, Augusta.' Philip sat back and removed his reading glasses. 'We've made an assumption the painting has something to do with Galloway's death because it's so valuable and went missing so suddenly. And if it has been stolen... well, that's the National Gallery's concern and not ours, isn't it?'

'We need to consider other possibilities,' said Augusta. 'Let's not forget Vanessa Curwen lied to us about when she last visited the National Gallery. Why? And there's Lillian Galloway too. She last saw her father a year ago and told us they weren't close.'

'You think his own daughter could have murdered him?' asked Philip.

'It's not a nice thought, but I think we have to consider it. Both Lillian Galloway and Vanessa Curwen are suspicious.'

'So is Cecil White-Thomas. But because we have to pretend we're some old friends of Edward's, we can't question them.' Philip clenched his jaw. 'It's so frustrating!'

Chapter Twenty-Five

'I THOUGHT I'd done an excellent job of repairing *The Wind in the Willows*,' said Fred the following morning. 'But there's a problem with it.'

'Problem?' said Augusta, admiring the burgundy cloth-bound volume in his hand. 'I can't see a problem with it. I think you're being a little too hard on yourself, Fred.'

'No I don't think I am.' He turned to the back of the book and flicked through the pages. 'Look at the page numbering. It's out of order. I muddled up some of the sections. Now the end of the book is about two thirds of the way in.'

Augusta gave an amused sigh. 'Oh dear. How annoying. And, apart from that, it looks so perfect too! You could have kept the mistake a secret from me and I never would have guessed just by looking at the book.'

'I think a customer would have complained before long.'

'Yes I suppose someone would have noticed soon enough. The challenge now is to take the book apart, put the sections in the right order and repair it again.' She grinned. 'I'm sure you can do it, Fred.'

He gave a sigh which suggested he wasn't so certain. 'I'll give it a try.'

'I have every confidence in you, Fred. And I need to ask you about magazines again. Do you know the names of any reputable poetry magazines?'

'First art and now poetry,' he said. 'The investigation you're working on at the moment sounds quite cultured.'

Augusta smiled. 'It might be. It depends how good the poetry is.'

'There's *The Gilded Quill* periodical,' said Fred. 'And *Temple of Verse* and *The Elysian Ledger* are quite good too.'

'Thank you, Fred. I'll pay a visit to the library and look them up.'

'Do you need to go now? If not, I can come with you later and help if you like.'

Augusta thought of all the journals she was going to have to look through. It could be a lot of work. 'If you could help me, Fred, I'd be really grateful. Thank you.'

They closed the shop a little earlier that day and headed to the library in High Holborn. It was an attractive stone building with tall arched windows. Augusta hoped they would find what they were looking for quickly, the library would be closing in an hour's time.

'I'll show you where the publications are kept,' said Fred, leading her through the quiet corridors.

In the periodicals section, magazines were displayed on racks. 'These are the most recent ones,' Fred whispered. 'If you're looking for something older, they're bound in volumes—just over there.' He pointed to a set of shelves lined with leather-bound editions, their spines gilded and slightly worn.

Augusta pulled out a volume of *The Gilded Quill*. 'We need to look for poems written by Lillian Galloway,' she said.

'Very well.' Fred pulled out one of the volumes for *Temple of Verse*. 'Let's see what we can find.'

'Thank you Fred,' she whispered as they carried their heavy volumes to a table. 'Two sets of eyes are better than one.'

Augusta leafed through each issue quickly but methodically, scanning headers and verse structures, growing familiar with the layout of the journal. She'd only been working for ten minutes when Fred found something.

'There's a poem here by Lillian Galloway,' he whispered.

'Well done!' She edged her chair closer to his and leaned in so she could read it:

He walked away,
   On a summer's day,
   No time to say,
   Goodbye.

   And now she's gone,
   With a doleful song,
   To sing along,
   Goodbye.

'Not very cheery,' said Augusta. 'I wonder who walked away? Her father?'

Fred pulled a grimace. 'It's not very good, is it? I'm surprised it got published in *Temple of Verse*.'

'Well it's got some rhythm to it,' said Augusta. 'And it rhymes.'

'I suppose so,' said Fred. 'I'll carry on searching for more masterpieces by Lillian Galloway.'

Augusta pulled out her notebook and copied down the lines, relieved the poem was short enough to transcribe quickly.

She turned to her own volume with renewed focus. They didn't have long before the library closed for the day. Her eyes grew weary as she quickly scanned each page. As time ticked by, she grew less and less hopeful that they'd find anything else. She knew they could return to the library another time, but she was impatient to understand a little more about Lillian Galloway.

'Here's another,' whispered Fred.

'Really?'

They were interrupted by the librarian ringing the closing bell and asking everyone to take their books to the desk or return them to the shelves.

Augusta shuffled up next to Fred and swiftly scribbled down the verse as the bell rang again and the overhead lights began to dim.

What do you hope to gain
By coming back here?
After you left us.
You may as well have left us for dead.
After all, isn't that what you did?
You assumed she'd always be here.
So did I.
But I was a child.

You knew better.
You knew life was fragile.
You knew nothing lasts forever.
How can a child comprehend such notions?
You should have been there.
But you weren't.

'It's even worse than the last one,' said Fred.

'It doesn't rhyme, does it?' replied Augusta as she frantically copied down the last few words. 'But poetry doesn't have to rhyme I suppose.'

'If it's not going to rhyme then it needs to be good.'

Augusta smiled. 'Even so, I think I can discern a common theme in these two poems. Abandonment.'

'There's definitely a strong sense of abandonment,' agreed Fred. 'Lillian Galloway appears to have a score to settle.'

The librarian appeared by their table. 'The library is closed now,' she said.

'Thank you, we're just leaving,' said Augusta, putting her notebook in her handbag. She picked up the volume to put it back on the shelf.

'No, leave it on the table,' instructed the librarian. 'I'll sort it out. People never put these back in the right place.'

Chapter Twenty-Six

'Abandonment,' said Philip once he'd read Lillian Galloway's poems. 'Yes I can see why you'd suggest that, Augusta. I can't claim to be an expert on poetry but it's clear from these poems that Miss Galloway feels aggrieved about someone who left her.'

They sat together in the easy chairs in Philip's office. It was dark outside but the fire in the grate cast warm flickering shadows on the walls.

'A woman and a man are referenced in these poems,' Augusta said. 'Lillian's parents, perhaps? We know Galloway was widowed so the lines "And now she's gone" and "You assumed she'd always be here" could refer to Lillian's mother and her death.'

'Did Galloway walk out on them?' asked Philip. 'Because that's what I sense from these. "He walked away, On a summer's day" and "After you left us. You may as well have left us for dead."'

'It's possible,' said Augusta. 'But I don't know for sure.'

'If he did leave his wife and daughter then it explains

why Lillian didn't see much of him before his death. She could have been angry at him. These poems seem angry, don't they?'

Augusta nodded. 'They do. I just wish we'd had more time in the library today so Fred could find some more.'

'Well if all Lillian's poetry is written with the same sentiment then I think these poems are useful enough.' He sat back in his chair. 'Is it good poetry?'

'Fred doesn't think so,' said Augusta.

Philip frowned. 'You've told Fred about our investigation?'

'No. I only asked him to help me find Lillian's poems. And besides… even if he did get an inkling of what we're working on, I know we can trust him to keep it quiet.'

He gave a nod. 'Yes, I trust him too.'

'And regarding Lillian's poetry, I'm no expert,' said Augusta. 'It doesn't strike me as particularly talented poetry. It's not evocative is it? And there don't appear to be any hidden meanings or metaphorical references. It just reads as if a young woman harbouring anger and sadness has put her thoughts on the page.'

'Which she has,' said Philip. 'Perhaps that's classed as good poetry these days? I wouldn't know. All I do know is that I studied a bit of Keats at school and it was a little more wordy than this.'

He pulled off his reading glasses, gave a large sigh and ran a hand through his hair.

Augusta sensed something was bothering him. 'What's wrong?' she asked.

'This investigation. We can't do anything, can we?'

'What do you mean? I think we've done quite a bit already and Fred did an excellent job today of finding some of Lillian Galloway's poetry.'

'Yes, he did. And I certainly don't mean to diminish his work. What we've done so far is good, but our hands are tied, aren't they? I would like to ask Lillian Galloway about her relationship with her father and I'd like to find out if she has an alibi for the night he was poisoned. And as for Vanessa Curwen, I want to ask her lots of questions and find out what she's hiding. The same goes for Cecil White-Thomas. But we can't, can we? Not while we're working undercover. In fact, I've a good mind to tell Wetherell that we can't do anything more.'

Augusta felt surprised to hear this. She'd assumed Philip would be happy to continue working until they made a breakthrough. 'I agree it's not easy,' she said. 'But we know we're onto something, don't we? We know Miss Curwen lied and there's something funny about the painting which was removed from Galloway's office and—'

'Yes but we can't investigate it properly, can we? We have no authority. And I can guarantee you, Augusta, that if we ask any of our suspects any more questions then they'll become suspicious that we're not who we say we are. I really don't think I'm prepared to do much more on this without Wetherell giving us a bit more.'

'A bit more what?'

'Information! Or the authority to properly bring people in for questioning. I want to put them on the spot and see how they respond.'

'That's because you're used to doing things that way, Philip.'

'Absolutely.' He folded his arms and gave a firm nod.

'I think we'll get there,' said Augusta. 'I'm used to investigating things slowly and carefully.'

'I'm afraid it's too slow for me,' said Philip. 'Too frustrating. I'm going to tell Wetherell that we've done all we can for now.'

'I see.' Augusta felt her shoulders slump. Could this mean they'd stop the investigation altogether? 'What if Wetherell asks someone else to investigate instead of us?'

Philip shrugged. 'So be it. They're welcome to it. I'm tired of being boring Roger Parker.'

'I don't like giving up on an investigation.'

'This isn't giving up, Augusta. With a bit of luck, Wetherell will give us something more when I tell him. Then we can resume our work.'

'And how are you going to tell him? We don't even know where to find him. He told us they don't know him in Whitehall.'

'He'll call on us sooner or later.'

'So we do nothing now and wait until he turns up again?'

Philip nodded. 'Although we could go to a nice restaurant tonight for dinner. What do you think?'

Augusta smiled. 'I'd like that.' She picked up her handbag and got to her feet. 'And can we agree on something?'

'What's that?' Philip stepped over to the cloak stand to fetch his coat.

'While we're there, we're not allowed to talk about the case.'

He draped his coat over his arm and gave her a kiss. 'That's absolutely fine by me.'

'Oh... and I almost forgot. Lady Hereford is hosting a tea party in her suite at the Russell Hotel tomorrow. You will come, won't you?'

Philip's shoulders slumped. 'Must I?'

'Yes. Fred and I are worried we'll be the only people there.'

'And what's wrong with that?'

'Everything! We need more people. Oh, please come.'

He put on his hat. 'Very well. But only if you pay for dinner tonight.'

'No, dinner was your idea.'

Philip laughed and shook his head. 'Come on. If we stand about here bickering, there won't be any good tables left.'

Chapter Twenty-Seven

THE FOLLOWING MORNING, Owen Ridley adjusted a chipped ceramic figurine in a dusty cabinet by his shop door. Through the grimy windowpane, he spotted a woman pause outside on the pavement.

Vanessa Curwen.

He gave a weary tut and wandered to the back of the shop. Moments later, the bell above the door tinkled as she stepped inside. He busied himself with the brass telescope he'd been trying to reassemble all week.

'Mr Ridley,' she called. 'How are you?'

Her voice was smooth and she was immaculately dressed in a Tuscan red coat. The colour contrasted sharply with her green feline eyes.

'I'm well, thank you,' he replied coolly. 'What brings you here?'

'There's no need to be so standoffish, Ridley. Have I done something to offend you?'

'No. I'm not easily offended.'

But her presence irritated him. It seemed she appeared only when she needed something.

She examined the shelves, picking up objects with gloved fingers. She paused at a carved wooden box and turned it over, inspecting the worn base. 'I wonder if you might do me a favour, Ridley?' she said lightly.

'What sort of favour?'

'I've a buyer coming to view the painting *The Silent Road to Winter* at the gallery tomorrow. It would help if you were there, showing a little enthusiasm to push up the price. You know how it is, some admiration and the occasional phrase such as "masterful use of light".'

He raised an eyebrow. 'And how much will you pay me?'

'Would eight pounds suffice?'

'Ten.' It was a decent week's wages for some people.

She gave a tight smile. 'Very well. Ten. But no more than that.'

He felt she had some nerve quibbling over a few pounds. Her recent sales had made her extremely wealthy.

Ridley put down the telescope pieces and rested his hands on the back of a shabby, imitation Louis XV chair. 'I read in *The Art Chronicle* what you sold *The Melancholy of Saint Aurelia* for,' he said casually. 'A tidy sum.'

She adjusted her hat. 'Yes, well, Veridiano is very popular.'

'And if I hadn't found those sketchbooks, no one would've heard of him.'

'You were well compensated for those sketchbooks, Ridley. Let's not pretend otherwise.'

'Not nearly as well as you were for that painting.'

She gave a small shrug. 'It sold at auction. I didn't expect it to go so far above the reserve price. The matter was out of my hands and, besides, the money was shared with the family of the recluse who'd hoarded it in her house for decades.'

He gave a slow nod. Miss Curwen was clearly downplaying her success. An attempt, perhaps, to soften the blow of just how handsomely she'd profited.

'And besides,' she added, brushing a speck of dust from her cuff, 'don't forget the auction house takes their cut as well.'

Ridley gave a dry smile. 'Oh, I know how an auction works, Miss Curwen. I was attending auctions when you were still being wheeled about in a perambulator.'

Her eyes narrowed, the glint in them hardening. 'What do you want, Ridley?'

'I want to be paid fairly.'

She let out a sigh. 'You know how this world turns. When a new artist sparks interest, the prices rise. When you found those sketchbooks, who could have guessed Veridiano would become the darling of the salons? I understand your frustration, but people pay what they're willing to pay. I've lost money on plenty of paintings. It's a contrary game, and control is often an illusion.'

She spoke to him as if he were a newcomer to the world of art and collectibles. And yet he was old enough to be her father. Her superior, condescending manner irritated him. But he knew something which could cut her down to size. It would leave her puzzling about it for the rest of the day. 'What about Galloway?' he said.

Her nose twitched. 'What about him?'

'He had a Veridiano in his office when he died, didn't he? What's happened to it?'

'It's been loaned to a gallery in Florence.'

'Has it? It seems strange to me. There's been all this interest in Veridiano and yet the painting leaves the country.'

She gave a casual shrug. 'That's what Galloway arranged. I didn't agree with it, but I wasn't consulted. You know me—I'd have sold it if I could. But what's done is done.'

Ridley leaned in a little closer and lowered his voice. 'You do know there was something odd about Galloway's death, don't you?'

A flicker of unease crossed her face before smoothing over again.

'Odd? What do you mean?'

'I know one of the gallery's security guards. Decent fellow. He said they'd all been told to report anything unusual regarding him to the head of security. Apparently, Galloway had been receiving threats.'

Her eyebrows raised. 'Threats? Galloway never mentioned anything to me.'

'No, he wouldn't have. But security were under instruction. If anything happened to him, the head of security had to be told first. And so that's what happened that night when one of them found him dead at his desk. Doesn't that strike you as unusual?'

He watched her face clearly, interested to see her reaction. She paused, then said, 'A little, perhaps.'

'Do you believe it was a heart attack that carried him off?'

'Of course! Why wouldn't I?'

He shrugged. 'Interesting.'

'Why do you say that, Ridley? Are you suggesting it wasn't a heart attack?'

He shrugged. 'I don't know exactly what happened. But I'm certain there's something very strange going on at that gallery.'

Miss Curwen remained silent but her eyes were wide with concern. Either she was shocked by his suggestion or she was worried he'd found her out.

He wondered which it was.

Chapter Twenty-Eight

THE TURNOUT for Lady Hereford's tea party at the Russell Hotel was surprisingly large. A long table had been set up in the living area and was laden with tiered cake stands and delicate bone china. Bunting was pinned haphazardly to the curtains and the song *Roses of Picardy* piped noisily from a large gramophone.

Augusta stood near the window with a cup of tea, watching as Lady Hereford presided from her bath chair. She wore a mint green velvet turban decorated with peacock feathers and a matching dress.

'Fred!' she called. 'You must sit nearer the piano. If we can coax someone into playing, we'll be heard at the end of the corridor.'

'I don't play the piano,' Fred protested.

'No matter. Sit near it and look musical.'

'Have another sandwich, Mr Fisher!' Lady Hereford barked at Philip, who'd just taken a sip of tea.

'I've had four,' he replied.

'Then you clearly need a fifth. Augusta, pass him the plate, would you?'

Augusta did as instructed, catching Philip's eye and smiling as she did so.

'Is this all for the Dowager Lady Pontypool's benefit?' he asked.

'Yes,' said Augusta. 'Lady Hereford is keen to show her she hasn't been invited.'

Philip gave an exasperated sigh and bit into his fifth sandwich.

Augusta counted about thirty guests. They were smartly dressed, well-spoken and mostly over the age of sixty. A young French couple appeared to have stumbled across the party by accident and were sitting politely in the corner.

'Everybody, this is Mr Bathurst!' Lady Hereford pointed to an elderly gentleman standing by her bath chair. 'He's a retired barrister and he's going to recite some poetry!'

Philip gave a quiet groan. 'I hope it wasn't written by Lillian Galloway.'

Augusta choked on her tea and took refuge by a curtain to recover herself.

'Shall we turn the gramophone off?' shouted Mr Bathurst.

'No need, Jonathan. I think you'll do a perfectly good job talking over it!'

A knock at the door interrupted them. Lady Hereford grinned. 'I wonder who that could be? Someone complaining about the noise perhaps?'

Her nurse, Doris, answered the door and a bell boy stepped in with an envelope in his hand. 'A telegram for Mr Fisher,' he announced.

Augusta was taken aback. Who'd possibly known Philip was at the party?

Philip cleared his throat in surprise. 'Goodness. Thank

you.' He stepped forward and took the telegram from the boy. Everyone in the room watched as he did so.

'Right then,' said Lady Hereford, a little subdued. She'd clearly been disappointed the bell boy hadn't arrived with a complaint from the Dowager Lady Pontypool. 'Off you go then, Jonathan. We're all ears!'

The old man began with gusto, staring up at the high ceiling as he recited the words. After two lines, his voice faltered. 'I think it would be easier if we turned off the gramophone,' he said. *Home, Sweet Home* by Dame Nellie Melba was now playing.

Lady Hereford sighed. 'If you insist, Jonathan.'

The nurse stepped over to the gramophone and was just about to stop it when another knock at the door sounded.

'Ah ha!' said Lady Hereford. 'Surely this must be someone with a complaint.'

Augusta thought she looked rather pleased about it.

The nurse answered the door and a small, white-haired lady in pearls and a peacock blue dress stepped in. She carried a little Pomeranian dog in her arms.

Augusta realised she was the Dowager Lady Pontypool.

'Rosemary,' said Lady Hereford coolly. 'Is the noise bothering you?'

'No not really,' she replied with a smile. 'It sounds like you're all having a jolly old time though. Mind if I join you?'

She was friendlier than Augusta had expected and Lady Hereford seemed disarmed. With all her guests watching, she couldn't possibly be rude.

A smile broke out across Lady Hereford's face. 'Of course! Come and help yourself to tea and sandwiches.'

The gramophone continued to play and Mr Bathurst seemed to forget about his poetry recitation.

By the window, Philip showed Augusta the telegram he'd received. 'It's anonymous,' he said. 'But I think I can guess who it's from.'

The telegram simply read:

Seven Stars, seven o'clock.

Chapter Twenty-Nine

THE SEVEN STARS was in a narrow, dark street behind the imposing Gothic building of the Royal Courts of Justice. Dim lights glowed from the court's arched windows and Augusta pictured lawyers inside working late on complicated cases.

'Apparently this is one of the few pubs to have escaped the Great Fire of London,' said Philip.

Augusta surveyed the small simple brick building. 'I had no idea it was that old.'

Inside, the air was thick with tobacco smoke. The place had seen better days. Its wallpaper was yellowed and the wood panelling dulled with age.

Augusta and Philip made their way to a shadowed table in the far corner where a solitary man sat with a cigarette burning low between his fingers. Amber lamplight reflected on the lenses of his black-rimmed spectacles.

Wetherell didn't rise to greet them. He just gave a curt nod as they took their seats opposite him.

'It seems you've read my mind,' Philip said to him. 'I mentioned to Augusta only yesterday evening that I wanted to meet with you again to discuss Galloway's death. How did you know I was at a tea party at the Russell Hotel?'

Wetherell shrugged. 'There's no need to ask me superfluous questions, Fisher.'

Augusta sensed Philip bristling beside her. 'But we have other questions,' he said. 'And we need you to answer them. Otherwise, we can't continue with this investigation.'

Wetherell ground his cigarette into the ashtray with deliberate slowness. 'I doubt I'll be able to answer any of them.'

A pause followed. Wetherell was a frustrating person to deal with. As the tension grew between the two men, Augusta decided to break the silence and tell Wetherell how their investigation had been progressing. She explained the rediscovery of Veridiano and named the people they suspected. As she spoke, Wetherell lit another cigarette and stared at its smouldering tip, as if it held greater significance than anything she was saying.

'So,' Augusta finished, 'we have suspects. And possible motives. But we don't know if Galloway—Hastings—was killed because of the painting *Portrait of a Widow with a Lark* or for another reason.'

Wetherell said nothing and Augusta noticed Philip's hands ball with frustration. He leaned forward and lowered his voice. 'We all thought Hastings was **dead**. We knew he was captured in Belgium and we all knew how ruthless the enemy was with captured spies. How did he get out? How did he get back to England?'

'You know I can't answer that,' said Wetherell.

'He's dead now,' Philip snapped. 'Why can't you tell us? And there are the other agents who went missing in Belgium too. Lennox. Cavendish. Blake. Did they survive too?'

The mention of their names stirred a deep sadness within Augusta. She'd assumed they'd perished, just as she'd assumed Hastings had. Perhaps now there was renewed hope. But she suspected Wetherell wasn't going to tell them anything directly.

Wetherell gave a slow exhale of smoke. 'You're asking questions you know I won't answer.'

Philip shook his head, exasperated. 'Why did you even ask to meet us? If you're not going to help us, what's the point? We're running around in circles pretending to be old friends of Edward Galloway and we're supposed to ask questions about his death without ever implying there was anything unnatural about it. We're not police, we don't have any authority—and worst of all, if we're found out, this entire charade collapses.'

'You're doing well so far,' said Wetherell.

'We're not,' said Augusta, feeling her own frustration come to the surface. 'Our cover is wearing thin. Someone is going to put the pieces together and realise we're not who we're claiming to be. I'm sure Galloway's secretary, Miss Miller, is growing suspicious of us. And Cecil White-Thomas is fed up with us too.'

'That's unfortunate,' Wetherell said.

'Involve the police,' Philip said. 'Let them open a proper investigation. You can brief them confidentially and tell them what you told us.'

'I can't do that.'

'Why not?'

'Because Galloway's former identity must remain protected,' Wetherell said. 'Even in death.'

Philip let out a hollow laugh. 'You're protecting a ghost. And for what? Some old file gathering dust in Whitehall?'

'If his identity is revealed,' Wetherell said, ignoring

Philip's tone, 'it compromises the others who worked with him. Including you.' He rose from his seat. 'Excuse me,' he said. 'I'm just going to visit the cloakroom.'

He vanished into the smoky dimness.

'He has to be the most insufferable man I've ever met!' said Philip. 'I wish we'd never come here. We're wasting our time. When he returns I'm going to tell him that he can stick his investigation—'

'Wait,' interrupted Augusta. Her eyes had drifted to Wetherell's chair, where his raincoat was draped over the back. She stood up and swiftly stepped over to it.

'What are you doing?' Philip hissed.

'Looking in his pockets.'

Her heart pounded as she pushed her hands into the satin-lined pockets of the raincoat. Wetherell could return at any moment and she didn't like to think what the punishment could be for going through a senior agent's pockets.

She felt a spectacles case, a slim pocket book and a piece of card which felt like a train ticket. 'Keep watching out for him,' she whispered to Philip as she unfolded the coat slightly to reach the inner pockets.

Philip sat still and motionless, his eyes fixed in the direction Wetherell had walked off to.

Augusta's fingers fumbled with nerves as she pushed her hands into the inside pockets. Her palms felt clammy. Was this a foolish idea?

'Augusta, he'll be back any second—'

'I know.'

She came across a bunched-up handkerchief and recoiled a little before checking another pocket. Then she came across a folded piece of paper. She swiftly pulled it out and pushed it into the pocket of her skirt.

There was no time to search any longer. She stepped

away from the coat and was barely seated again when Wetherell returned with the same inscrutable look on his face. As he sat down, Augusta realised she hadn't quite refolded the coat as Wetherell had left it. Surely an agent of his experience would notice?

She took in a slow breath, trying to calm her thudding heart. What was the piece of paper she'd pulled out of the coat? She hoped it wasn't just a shopping list.

'Is there anything more you can tell us now?' Philip asked Wetherell.

'I'm not here to tell you anything I'm afraid. And I'm sorry you've found our conversation less than enlightening. But please be assured I've learned an enormous amount from the pair of you. That was, after all, the purpose of today's meeting. To gauge your progress.'

He got to his feet with slow precision, picked up his raincoat and put it on. Then he gave them both a nod. 'Keep going. You're doing well.'

Without another word, he turned and walked out.

Silence followed as they stared at the empty chair opposite them.

'Ridiculous,' muttered Philip. 'A complete waste of our time.'

'I hope it wasn't,' Augusta said, pulling the folded slip of paper from her pocket. She opened it out and placed it on the table between them.

Brussels. 51°33'13.8"N 0°06'46.1"W.

Philip put on his reading glasses and peered at it. 'Goodness. This looks interesting.'

Augusta smiled. 'I was worried it might be a list of groceries.'

'Brussels sprouts?' suggested Philip.

Augusta nudged him with her elbow. 'That's a terrible joke. These numbers look like coordinates.'

'We need a map. I've got a few in my office we can look at.' He turned to her. 'Do you mind working late this evening, Augusta?'

'Not at all. We need to find out what this means.'

Chapter Thirty

THE TRAFFIC on High Holborn was slow.

'What's the hold up?' Vanessa Curwen called out to the taxi driver.

'Blowed if I know,' he responded. 'Traffic gets worse every year. Whole of London will come to a standstill before long. None of us will be able to move.' He gave a wry chuckle.

Vanessa sighed and glanced out of the window. The shops were closed but lights glimmered from the public houses and restaurants. How nice it would be to enjoy one of these places with Cecil, but he had other plans this evening with his wife. She felt her teeth clench at the thought.

A street lamp cast a pool of light on a couple passing beneath it, arm-in-arm. The man was using a walking stick.

Vanessa caught her breath. There was something familiar about them. As the taxi crawled past, she turned to catch a glimpse of their faces.

Mr and Mrs Parker.

'Stop here please,' she said to the driver.

'I thought you wanted taking to Bloomsbury Square?'

'I've decided to walk the rest of the way.'

She paid him the fare as Mr and Mrs Parker walked past the car. Once they were a reasonable distance ahead, she slipped out of the taxi, heart quickening, and followed.

Their pace was slow as Mr Parker moved with the help of his stick. Vanessa patiently followed as they crossed Kingsway and continued on westwards.

A short while later, they stopped to cross the main road. Although it was dark, Vanessa stepped into the shadow of a doorway to be certain they wouldn't see her. Once they'd crossed, she hurried after and followed them into Bury Place.

Bloomsbury Square was close by, was it possible they were walking to her gallery? Or did they have other business in the area?

The street was quiet here and Vanessa did her best to remain in the shadows. Her shoes began to pinch her feet. They were the type of shoes which looked stylish but weren't designed for walking much distance.

Bury Street ended where it met Great Russell Street. On the other side of the street, the railings of the British Museum were just visible in the gloom. Mr and Mrs Parker turned right, walked a short distance, then stopped.

Mr Parker took something from his pocket, stepped up to a door and unlocked it. Did the Parkers live on a flat on this street?

Vanessa waited until the pair had stepped in through the door and disappeared from view. Then she cautiously walked up to the door they'd gone through. On the wall beside it was a small brass plaque. She could just make out the words in the light of a streetlamp: P. Fisher. Private Detective Agency.

Perhaps the building contained both offices and flats?

She stepped past the door to a bookshop with a tidy book display in the window.

A light suddenly glowed above her and she looked up to where a window above the shop was now lit. Presumably Mr and Mrs Parker were in the room.

Vanessa crossed the street and surveyed the building from the other side of the road. A bookshop with a door next to it which belonged to a private detective. And above the shop a room which Mr and Mrs Parker were now in. Their flat? Or the office of the private detective?

Whatever it was, it was only around the corner from her gallery in Bloomsbury Square. Vanessa gave a shiver. She had no idea they were so close to her.

She glanced up and down the street, wondering how she could find out more about the mysterious Mr and Mrs Parker. Opposite the museum was a well-lit public house. Vanessa headed for it in her uncomfortable shoes.

It was time to make some inquiries.

Chapter Thirty-One

AUGUSTA AND PHILIP sat in the easy chairs in his office and examined the coordinates on the slip of paper from Wetherell's pocket.

'Fifty-one and a half degrees north,' said Augusta. 'That's roughly the latitude for central London.'

Philip nodded. 'And this longitude coordinate... it places the location just west of the prime meridian. So somewhere west of Greenwich. Possibly north London, like Kentish Town or Hampstead.' He sat back for a moment. 'Well I'm relieved this appears to be a London location and not somewhere in the Outer Hebrides.'

'But what can Brussels mean?' said Augusta. 'I don't understand that part.'

'Perhaps there's a Brussels Street?' Philip got up from his seat and stepped over to his shelves. 'Here's the most recent Ordnance Survey map I have for London.' He took it over to the table by the window and unfolded the large sheet. 'The scale is one inch to one mile. It's not enormously detailed, but it should give us a rough idea of where the location falls.'

Augusta joined him at the table and smoothed out the map. 'The coordinates seem to place the location north of the river and west of Greenwich. That should be somewhere around here.' She traced a wide, looping circle with her fingertip.

'A densely populated area,' Philip said, his brow furrowing. 'That won't narrow it down easily. But this map has a grid.' He paused, smiling faintly. 'Can you remember how to convert latitude and longitude into Ordnance Survey grid references, Augusta?'

She returned his smile, quietly confident. 'I think I can remember the steps. Although it's been a few years, hasn't it?'

Maps had been essential to their work during the war —both reading them and creating them.

'I like to think I remember how it's done,' said Philip. 'But let's not take any chances. Do you still have a copy of the guide?'

'Yes, it's in a drawer in my workshop. I'll go and fetch it.'

Downstairs, the dark shop felt eerily quiet. Augusta could just see enough to find her way to her workshop and, once inside, she flicked on the light. It was harsh and dazzling but the piles of books awaiting repair were a familiar, comforting sight.

As she looked through the drawers to find the conversion guide, she felt a prickle on the back of her neck. Stopping, she straightened and glanced around. There was no one else in here but it felt like there was.

She caught her reflection in the window which overlooked the yard at the back. Her workshop blazed with light while outside everything was dark. She'd long intended to get a curtain for the window but had reasoned no one could ever get into the yard to look in.

Or had she been mistaken?

She shrugged off the sense of foreboding and returned to her task. Once she'd found the guide, she turned off the light and was struck by how little she could see. With halting steps, she made her way back across the shop to the staircase.

Her body felt tense, like a coiled spring. And she felt an overwhelming sensation of being watched. She told herself she was mistaken and climbed back up the stairs to Philip.

Moments later, Augusta sat at Philip's desk with the guide, her notebook and a freshly sharpened pencil. She began working through the conversion, carefully cross-referencing the numbers. The pencil scratched steadily against the paper.

Philip peered over her shoulder. 'Do you need any help?'

'Yes,' she replied without looking up. 'I need a strong cup of tea.'

'Very well.' He went into an adjoining room and the kettle whistled as Augusta worked, checking and rechecking her calculations until she felt certain.

When she finally had a grid reference, she got up and examined the map. 'I think I've got it,' she said, marking a little cross with her pencil. 'Lower Holloway.'

Philip adjusted his glasses and bent over the table, cup of tea in hand. 'There?'

'Yes. Near Holloway Road Tube station. Do you know it around there?'

'Not very well. But it's not far—an easy trip by tube or cab. It's not Wetherell's house, is it?'

Augusta laughed. 'Why would Wetherell be carrying around the coordinates for his home in his pocket?'

Philip shrugged. 'I wouldn't put it past him. He's a strange man. He could have just given us the piece of paper directly.'

'Not if he's not allowed to,' said Augusta.

'Ah.' Realisation dawned on Philip's face. 'He's forbidden to tell anyone about this mysterious place, but if someone happens to discover its existence then he can't be held responsible.'

'Yes, that must be the reason,' said Augusta.

Philip took a sip of tea. 'So tomorrow we should go and have a look, but…'

'What?'

'How does this have anything to do with our investigation?'

'We don't know yet,' said Augusta. 'It's an obscure lead but I think we should at least see what's there. And think about why he left the table for those few minutes.'

Philip's eyes narrowed. 'You think he did that deliberately? He knew you were going to go through his pockets?'

'He could have worn his coat, but he'd taken it off and left it with us. I think he wanted us to find that slip of paper.'

Philip grinned. 'I can't believe it's taken me this long to catch up with you, Augusta. Now that you've explained it, it makes sense. Although Wetherell appeared to be unhelpful, he was leading us to this.' He shook his head in admiration. 'Why on earth are you running a bookshop, Augusta? You should be working for the Secret Intelligence Service.'

Chapter Thirty-Two

THE BIOGRAPHY of Giovanni di Luca Veridiano was almost complete. Cecil White-Thomas smiled to himself as he leafed through his notes. They were going to look marvellous once his secretary had typed everything up neatly.

It wasn't a long biography, but centuries had passed since Veridiano's death and there were limited sources. Cecil felt sure he'd done as well as he possibly could.

A knock sounded at the door and his secretary stepped in. 'Miss Curwen is here to see you, sir.'

He felt his shoulders slump. What did Vanessa want now? Her visits to his workplace were becoming more frequent. People were going to start talking soon if she wasn't careful.

'Very well,' he said irritably. 'Show her in.'

Vanessa looked beautiful as always, wearing an indigo outfit which was probably by a French designer. She perched on the chair opposite him and gave him a wide smile.

'I don't have much time,' he said once his secretary had left the room. 'I've got to get this biography finished.'

Her smile faded. 'So that means you don't have time to hear all about Mr and Mrs Parker?'

'Galloway's dull, long-lost friend? I can't say I'm terribly interested in him.'

'Well that's a shame.' Vanessa got up from her chair. 'Because I've found out who he really is.'

'Who he really is?' The remark puzzled Cecil. 'What do you mean?'

'I mean what I say.' She headed for the door.

'Who is he?'

'You don't have much time, remember? You're trying to finish the biography.' She turned the door handle and opened the door.

He jumped to his feet. 'Vanessa!' he pleaded, leaning on his desk. 'Tell me about Parker.'

She slowly turned and gave him an imperious smile. 'Oh, so you do have some time after all?'

'I didn't realise you had something to tell me.'

'Why else do you think I would call on you, Cecil? For fun?'

'No.' Now he had to play along with her game and say the right things to get the information he wanted to hear. He ground his teeth silently and sat down again.

Vanessa closed the door and languorously made her way back to his desk, her expression smug.

'So who is he?' he asked impatiently.

He had to wait until she'd seated herself, placed her handbag by her chair, smoothed her skirt and crossed her legs.

'Mr Fisher,' she replied.

'And who's he?'

'A private detective. And his wife isn't his wife at all. Her name is Mrs Peel. She owns a bookshop and works as a lady detective when the mood takes her.'

Cecil felt a chill run through him. 'They're both detectives?'

'Yes.' Vanessa examined her nails. 'He once worked at Scotland Yard.'

'Scotland Yard?' Cecil's breath quickened. His mouth felt dry. 'Are you sure about this, Vanessa? How do you know?'

'I saw them last night on High Holborn. I followed them to Mrs Peel's bookshop, it's very near Bloomsbury Square. Mr Fisher's office is above it.'

'You spoke to them?'

'Oh no. I'm not that foolish, Cecil. No, I watched them go into the office and then I made some inquiries at a nearby public house, The Museum Tavern.'

'I know the place.'

'The handsome landlord there knows Mrs Peel and Mr Fisher. A pleasant chat with him told me everything.'

Cecil sat back in his chair and sighed. 'So they've been pretending to be old friends of Galloway's? Why?'

'I don't know. But I suspect they smell a rat, Cecil.' Her feline eyes held his gaze. 'Perhaps you haven't been careful enough.'

He felt a snap of irritation. 'Oh I've been careful, alright. But what about you? Who've you been talking to?'

She said nothing for a moment, leaving an uncomfortable silence to grow between them. When she spoke, her voice was low. The tone almost menacing. 'I've not been speaking to anyone, Cecil. You know me, I'm extremely discreet in all matters. Now you need to decide what we do next.'

He gave a laugh. 'Me?'

'Yes, Cecil. You. After all, this was all your idea.'

Chapter Thirty-Three

AUGUSTA AND PHILIP stepped out of Holloway Road tube station and paused to take in their surroundings.

The morning was grey and chilly and the busy street quite ordinary. It was lined with plain-looking shops for everyday living: groceries, shoe repairs and household wares. The road served as a route from the City of London to the north. A bus trundled past, making way for a rattling tram. Just south of the tube station a railway bridge crossed the road, its bricks darkened by soot and smoke.

'I wonder where the exact location can be,' said Philip, glancing around. 'It can't be the tube station itself, can it?' They turned to survey the building behind them with its arched windows and distinctive oxblood red tiles from the Edwardian era.

'I don't think it can be the station,' said Augusta. 'Let's think about what Wetherell wasn't telling us.'

'Pretty much everything,' Philip muttered.

'Exactly. He refused to answer your questions about how Hastings escaped capture. He told us nothing about Lennox, Cavendish and Blake. And yet he must know those details could be important to the case. So he's led us to a place where he can give us that information—just not directly.'

'An ordinary street in north London?' Philip glanced around doubtfully.

'It's more than that,' Augusta said. 'Wetherell must want us to use our initiative.'

She looked about them and her interest was drawn to the other side of the road, to a gap between the row of shops and the railway bridge. In the gap, there appeared to be an entrance to a scruffy yard. Hemmed in by brick walls and the railway line.

Philip followed her gaze. 'Ah ha,' he said. 'Railway arches. Often used for workshops and storage.'

They crossed the street, dodging a passing delivery van, and slipped through a rusted gate hanging half-open. In the yard, scrap metal and broken pieces of timber were heaped in piles against the wall. Above them was a large, faded advertisement for Player's Navy Cut Tobacco which had been painted onto the side of the building decades previously.

The ground was stony and uneven. Beneath the railway line, the arches were occupied by shuttered units. Augusta noticed each one had a number painted on it. The arch at the far end was the only one with its door open, the sound of hammering came from within.

'So what now?' said Augusta.

'I suppose we can ask the chap making that din,' said Philip.

They stepped cautiously over puddles and made their towards the open door.

'Excuse me!' Philip called out. From the dingy depths, a bearded man emerged from the cave-like workshop. He wore grimy blue overalls and a cigarette hung from his lip. He stared at them expectantly but saying nothing.

'Good morning,' Philip said. 'I wonder if you can help us. I'm Mr Fisher, and this is Mrs Peel.'

His eyes moved between them and still he said nothing.

'Are any of these units used for storage?' Philip asked.

The man shrugged.

Philip gave Augusta a weary glance. She thought of the slip of paper with the coordinates on it. There had been a word written there too.

A thought came to her and she was almost ready to dismiss it. After all, it was possible they'd come to the wrong place.

She cleared her throat and decided to try anyway. 'Does the word Brussels mean anything to you?' she asked the man.

His expression didn't change, but he reached into a pocket and drew out a small key attached to a battered luggage label. He held it out silently.

Augusta accepted the key. The number four was written on the label in heavy pencil.

'Thank you,' Philip said. 'That's very kind of you.'

The man stepped back into his workshop and Augusta and Philip walked along the row of arches to number four.

'What quick thinking, Augusta!' whispered Philip. 'Brussels was the code word! Now we're really onto something, I can't wait to see what's inside this arch.'

Augusta's pulse quickened as they approached number four. 'I really hope this helps us,' she said. 'We need some answers, don't we?'

'Yes we do.'

Her hand trembled as she fitted the key into the lock.

Chapter Thirty-Four

As the door creaked open, a blade of pale daylight sliced into the gloom, falling across a row of dented metal filing cabinets. Augusta and Philip cautiously stepped inside.

The air was cold and damp, heavy with the scent of rust and mildew. Above them, the rhythmic thunder of an approaching train became a deafening roar which rattled the brick structure around them. Augusta felt her shoulders relax as the noise diminished and relative peace returned.

'It's a shame we haven't brought a torch,' Philip muttered, his voice low in the darkness.

'I always carry a torch.' Augusta felt for it in her handbag and pulled it out. She switched it on and its narrow beam of light cut through the shadows and swept across the metal cabinets.

'Excellent, Augusta!' Philip said. He eased the door shut behind them, cutting off the last of the daylight. The storage unit seemed small and claustrophobic.

They stepped over to the nearest filing cabinet and Philip pulled out a drawer which opened with an uncomfortable screech. Inside were rows of manila folders, their tabs faded and dog-eared.

'Files,' he said quietly. 'A lot of them.'

He tugged out a file. Stamped in heavy black ink across the cover was a single word: confidential.

Augusta leaned in, shining the torch onto the papers as Philip leafed through the file. The pages were dense with typed reports, some bearing official stamps, others marked with handwritten annotations in faded blue ink. 'Well,' Philip said, 'these look like War Office files to me. Military Intelligence. Stored beneath a railway line in north London. Who would ever think to look here?'

Augusta shone her torch over the rows of filing cabinets. 'There are a lot here,' she said. 'And there are some cupboards over there too. It's going to take a long time to look through it all.'

'We're not here to investigate every file in the archive,' said Philip. 'We just need to find everything we can about Hastings. And the fates of Lennox, Cavendish and Blake too.'

They set to work. Pulling out files and quickly returning them when they didn't contain the information they were looking for. The torch beam darted back and forth, catching glimpses of old photographs paperclipped to reports, maps with hand-drawn notations and official letters. Every file held fragments of forgotten lives and missions conducted in secret. These files had once been critical to wartime strategy and now they were little more than relics.

Hours passed and trains thundered overhead. Augusta and Philip paused for breaks, taking occasional turns in the puddle-filled yard.

The task began to feel daunting.

'Wetherell could at least have put another clue on the

piece of paper,' said Augusta. 'A name or number of a file perhaps.'

'He doesn't like to be too helpful,' said Philip. 'He wants us to put the work in.'

Augusta sighed. 'We're doing that alright.' She paused to rub her eyes. They were tired from peering at old reports in torchlight. 'It must be lunchtime soon,' she added. 'I'm hungry.'

'We can't eat until we've found something useful,' said Philip.

'What?' Augusta turned to him in the gloom. 'That's unreasonable! You're almost as bad as Wetherell.'

'No, I'm not that bad.'

Augusta returned a file to its drawer and pulled out another with a sigh. She had a headache and her stomach gave a grumble as she turned the pages.

Then she felt a flip of excitement. 'Here!' she said. 'I've found Hastings' file!'

Chapter Thirty-Five

AUGUSTA'S PULSE quickened as she opened the folder and leafed through the pages. Philip stood by her, holding the torch.

'Here's a report detailing his capture,' she said, her eyes racing across the text. 'The date was the twelfth of March 1917. Hastings was apprehended by German military patrols on the riverfront in Dinant after delivering encoded materials disguised as a canvas painting. It says he was held for nine days. He claimed to have escaped during a prisoner transfer on the twenty-first of March.'

Augusta paused, breath catching as her gaze fell on the next lines. Her heart gave a sickening lurch. 'Oh no...'

'What is it?'

She read aloud, aware her voice sounded unsteady. '"Within seventy-two hours of subject's capture, German forces arrested operatives E Blake, mapping, V Lennox, wireless, and M Cavendish, cryptography. Rapid timing suggests actionable intelligence was provided to the enemy."'

Her words echoed in the cold, silent space.

Philip dropped the torch onto the file and drew a sharp breath. Then he gave a heavy exhale, the sound tight with anger. 'So Hastings betrayed them.'

Augusta gave a faint nod, throat constricting. 'I suppose... he must have feared for his life.'

'Of course he did!' Philip snapped, pacing the concrete floor. His footsteps rang harshly in the enclosed space. 'But that doesn't excuse it! We all understood the risks. Capture was always a possibility but we had rules. We swore an oath! To negotiate your freedom by sacrificing three others... that's not just cowardice. That's a death sentence for your own comrades!'

Augusta bowed her head, fingers tightening around the folder. She could see their faces—Lennox, Cavendish and Blake. Brave, clever people. 'You're right,' she whispered. 'It was unforgivable.'

She picked up the torch, cleared her throat and related the rest of the report to Philip. 'Hastings resurfaced near Comines on the twenty-fourth of March. He reported to Handler Jones with an account of his supposed escape. The report notes, "Physical condition good. No signs of injury or duress."'

She heard Philip's footsteps stop. 'No signs of injury?' His tone was incredulous. 'So he wasn't tortured? He gave them names freely. Just like that?'

They took another break from their work out in the yard. Augusta didn't feel hungry anymore. Her appetite had left her.

A light drizzle began to fall and Philip shifted uneasily from one foot to another. 'I'm feeling a pain in my leg today,' he said. 'Usually it's fine. It could be because we're being taken back to those days again. The days we tried so hard to forget.'

Augusta felt a heavy tug in her chest. She took his cold

hand and gave it a squeeze. 'We don't have to do this, Philip. We can just decide to stop.'

'No.' He shook his head. 'I want to finish this now. Let's go back in there and see if we can find out what happened to Lennox, Cavendish and Blake. I really want to find out if they survived like Hastings did.'

They worked side by side in the dim torchlight, opening drawer after drawer, sifting through faded records. Most of the files led nowhere—old surveillance reports and long-forgotten missions. Names they didn't recognise. Cases that no longer mattered.

But then, as Augusta replaced yet another useless folder, Philip's voice cut through the silence.

'I've got something.'

She looked up at once, pulse quickening. Philip held up a file. 'A list of agents who went missing during 1917.' He paused, opening it carefully. 'I turned to March—and this is what I found.' He tapped the page. 'Here's Edmund Blake. Cover identity, delivery man.' He cleared his throat and began to read aloud: '"Arrested March 1917 after betrayal by compromised asset, Hastings. Executed by German military authorities following refusal to divulge further operatives. Witness reports confirm he declined blindfold and maintained operational silence under interrogation."'

A chill rippled through Augusta. 'Oh goodness,' she whispered. 'Such a brave young man.'

'A contrast to Hastings, wouldn't you say?' Philip's voice was edged with bitterness.

Augusta nodded, tears pricking at her eyes. Young Edmund Blake. She could still picture him—the hopeful glimmer in his eyes, his quick smile. He'd wanted to be an actor. He'd looked younger than his twenty-three years and had always managed to make them laugh, even during the darkest days. A tear slipped down her cheek.

'Go on,' she whispered. 'What about Lennox?'

Philip scanned the page, voice lowering. '"Captured March 1917 following intelligence breach linked to Hastings. Blood trace discovered at capture site, body never recovered. German records suggest possible escape during prisoner transfer, however, no verified sightings post-1917. Presumed killed during escape attempt or executed covertly.'

'So he could still be alive?' Augusta asked, but as the words left her mouth, hope wavered.

'It's possible,' Philip said, 'but... I think the intelligence services would have known by now. If he'd survived, there would be an addendum to this file.'

Augusta swallowed a lump in her throat. She remembered Victor Lennox clearly—a quiet, gentle man. He'd built the wireless sets they used in Belgium. She could still hear him saying, 'Machines are easier than people. They don't lie.'

'And Cavendish?' Augusta asked. 'Please tell me she fared better.'

Philip turned the page. 'Shall I read it?'

'Yes.' Augusta steadied herself, bracing for what might come.

'"Arrested March 1917. Interned at Liège. Later transferred to Switzerland following Red Cross intervention. Returned to Britain 1918.'

Augusta's heart leapt. 'She survived?'

Philip hesitated before continuing. '"Physical recovery achieved, psychological effects persistent. Deceased 1921, pneumonia."'

Augusta closed her eyes. 'So she survived... but she suffered.'

They stood in silence for a moment.

Mabel Cavendish's face came back to her. Sharp, intelligent eyes. Mabel had once joked she could argue fluently in six languages. She'd always carried herself with quiet confidence. Hastings had betrayed her too. And although Mabel had lived through the war, the scars had followed her home.

The cold dampness seemed to press in around them now, as thick as the grief Augusta felt tightening in her chest.

'I need to get out of here,' she said, her breath quickening. 'I need air.'

Philip placed the file back in its drawer. 'Me too.'

He touched her shoulder, offering silent comfort, and together they stepped back out into the grey drizzle. A train thundered above them, drowning out all other sound.

Augusta inhaled deeply. 'So much loss,' she murmured. 'And all because of Hastings.'

Chapter Thirty-Six

'THANK YOU, MR RIDLEY,' said Vanessa Curwen. 'I don't think *The Silent Road to Winter* would have fetched that price without your help.' She handed him a wad of twenty ten-shilling notes. To her annoyance, he counted them carefully before pushing the bundle into his waistcoat pocket.

'You felt the need to count them?' she remarked. 'You don't trust me?'

He smirked. 'I don't think many of us trust each other in this business, do we?'

His comment wounded her a little. 'I trust people,' she retorted.

Ridley shrugged. 'That's your look out, I suppose.'

He turned to leave her gallery, but she tugged at his arm.

'What is it?' He looked her up and down, smirking again. Was he wondering if she wanted to seduce him?

Vanessa spoke quickly, keen to show it wasn't her intention at all. 'Tell me what you heard from the security guard,' she said. 'About Galloway.'

He looked away. 'I've told you all I know.'

'What sort of threats did he receive?'

'Some letters, apparently.'

'Saying what?'

'I don't know. And the security chap doesn't know either.'

'And the security guards were told to tell the head of security if anything happened to Galloway?' she asked.

'That's what I heard.'

'And you don't think Galloway died from a heart attack?'

'I don't know. I just think it's all a bit unusual. With that and the Veridiano in his office suddenly sent off to Italy.'

'Galloway arranged that.'

Ridley shook his head. 'He wouldn't have done.'

Vanessa clenched her jaw. 'What makes you so sure?'

'I just know he wouldn't have done it.' He stared at her over his pince nez and she stared back, not wanting to be the first to break the gaze. What did Ridley know? And did he suspect her of something?

She felt her shoulders tense, she couldn't bear the way his eyes bored into hers. Her breath quickened. Was it possible she'd underestimated him?

The gallery door opened and she gasped at the sudden noise.

A tall, lean bespectacled man stepped inside.

'Mr White-Thomas,' she said, as professionally as possible. As far as Ridley was concerned, she and Cecil were merely acquaintances.

'Good afternoon Miss Curwen. And Mr Ridley.' He gave them both a cursory nod.

'Afternoon Mr White-Thomas,' said Ridley. 'Miss Curwen and I were just discussing the Veridiano which was sent off to Italy. A bit strange, don't you think?'

Cecil gave an awkward laugh. 'Yes, very odd. But that was Galloway for you. Quite unpredictable.'

'Was he?' said Ridley. 'I didn't think he was like that.'

'Well if you'd worked closely with him—as I did—then you'd have soon realised it. The man had many quirks.'

Ridley said nothing, merely giving Cecil a pointed glance. Then he did the same to Vanessa. She shifted from one foot to the other, willing him to leave.

'Very well,' said Ridley. 'Pleasure doing business with you Miss Curwen.'

She felt her shoulders relax a little as he took his hat from the hat stand and stepped out of the door.

'What did he want?' Cecil asked once Ridley had gone.

'He helped me sell a painting,' replied Vanessa, still watching the door.

'That's nice of him.'

'I paid him for his time.

'And that's nice of you.'

She leant in and gave him a kiss. Then she turned and walked over to her desk, knowing he'd follow.

'So what brings you here?' she said over her shoulder. She knew he'd probably spent the day worrying about Mr Fisher and Mrs Peel.

'I've come up with a plan,' he replied.

'Is that right?' She settled into her chair behind her desk and rested her chin on one hand. 'And what's your plan, Cecil?'

He took off his jacket, put it on the back of the chair and sat down.

'We need to play them at their own game.'

She leaned in, intrigued. 'How do we do that?'

'We get rid of them.'

She froze. 'Cecil... you don't mean—?'

He gave a low chuckle. 'Not murder, darling. That

would be messy and difficult to explain. No, we just need to get them out of the way. Discredited. Preferably arrested.'

Vanessa let out a breath, her heartbeat steadying again. 'Arrested? For what?'

'Well that's where the fun begins.' He had a gleam in his eye. 'If we can frame Fisher for something—something serious—he'll never work again. Not in that field. And as for Mrs Peel—well, a scandal involving theft wouldn't sit well with the kind of clientele who frequent her bookshop.'

Vanessa laughed. 'Oh Cecil, that's deliciously wicked. But clever.' She picked up her silver cigarette case. 'What do you have in mind?'

'I've thought it through. The gallery has a Titian in storage at the moment, *Venus and Adonis*. We removed it from display a few weeks ago during the reorganisation. It's sitting quietly in the storeroom.'

'And?' She offered him a cigarette but he shook his head.

'We report it as stolen.'

'Stolen?'

'Yes. We hide it. Temporarily misplace it. The gallery won't miss it for long. Trust me. We'll make sure the theft gets linked to Fisher and Peel. The fact that they've been snooping around, asking questions, nosing into things they shouldn't… well, it won't be hard to spin a story from that. Once the police start looking, they'll uncover the truth we plant for them.'

Vanessa lit her cigarette and smiled. 'It would be quite the scandal,' she said. 'Former Scotland Yard inspector and respectable shopkeeper caught red-handed with a stolen Titian.'

'Precisely. The press will be delighted.'

'And once they're discredited, no one will believe a word they say about Veridiano or anything else.'

He leaned back with satisfaction. 'Then we can return to business as usual—without their interference.'

Vanessa blew out a long stream of smoke. 'Oh Cecil… remind me never to cross you. So how are we going to carry out the plan?'

He lowered his voice, even though there was no one else around to hear. 'I'll remove the canvas from its frame, roll it up and place it in a secure box. Then I'll take the box to a storage depository in Shoreditch. I know just the one. It's run by a removals firm called C White and they're used to storing high-value items.'

'Will it be safe there?' she asked.

'As safe as it needs to be,' he replied. 'I'll make sure it's stored in one of their secure rooms, and I'll tell them it's a valuable family heirloom. But here's the fun part—when I make the arrangements, I'll give them a false name.'

'What name?'

'Philip Fisher.' Cecil smiled.

Vanessa burst into laughter. 'Oh, Cecil. You're devilish!'

'I do try. Then, once the painting is safely stored, Mr Fisher will receive an anonymous note directing him to collect a lost item from that address on a specific day and time. At the same time, another anonymous note will arrive at Scotland Yard, tipping them off that the stolen Titian is hidden at that same location.'

'And they'll turn up and find him there?'

'Exactly. With Mrs Peel too. They'll both be caught.'

'Do you think they'll go?'

'Oh, I'm certain of it. They won't be able to resist.'

'And the police will catch them red-handed with the stolen painting in their possession.'

'Precisely.'

'But will the police really believe it's them? Won't they think it's a setup?'

Cecil gave her a cool smile. 'How will Fisher explain his presence at the exact location of a missing Titian? What possible excuse could he offer? And Mrs Peel—what will she say? That they were invited by a mysterious stranger? It'll sound like a feeble attempt to deflect guilt.'

Vanessa inhaled on her cigarette as she thought. 'But what if someone at the storage firm remembers you and realises you're not the real Philip Fisher?'

He shrugged. 'That's a risk. But I'll space it out—leave a few days between dropping off the painting and the retrieval. People come and go from these places constantly. I'll dress inconspicuously and look as dull and forgettable as possible.'

Vanessa laughed. 'Don't say that, Cecil! You're anything but forgettable.'

'Thank you, darling.'

She grinned. 'It's a dangerous plan.'

'It's a perfect plan,' Cecil said.

'And what about Ridley?'

He frowned. 'What about him?'

'We're going to need a plan for him before long. He's questioning things.'

'What things?'

'He knows a security guard at the gallery who told him Galloway had been receiving threatening letters.' She watched his face but his expression remained impassive. 'Ridley is even wondering if Galloway didn't die of a heart attack after all.'

Cecil gave a laugh. 'So what's his theory then?'

She stubbed out her cigarette in her Murano glass ashtray. 'He didn't suggest anything specific but he thinks

Galloway's death and the missing Veridiano are both suspicious.'

'I see. And that's why he mentioned the Veridiano to me when I arrived here.'

'People are going to realise it's not in Italy before long, Cecil.'

'Maybe they will. But we can explain it away with the delivery going wrong. It got lost during transport and then it was found again.'

'And people will believe that?'

'Of course! You know how well-respected I am, Vanessa. Why would anyone doubt my word?'

'Very well.' She knew she had to trust him. She picked up her compact mirror and applied a layer of crimson lipstick. 'And we need another plan too, Cecil,' she said once she'd checked her appearance in her mirror.

His brow furrowed. 'For what?'

She got up from her seat and walked around her desk to where he sat. Then she perched herself on his lap. 'A plan for you to leave your wife, Cecil.'

'Oh that.' He looked away, his response disappointingly dismissive.

'But don't you think it's time? You keep telling me you don't love her anymore.'

'Let's just get all this business out of the way first, Vanessa.'

He was putting it off again. It was almost a year since he'd first said he would leave Margaret.

'I'm tired of being a secret, Cecil!'

'I know you are, darling.' He turned back to her. 'But don't you think it's fun being a secret?'

'It was to begin with. But not anymore.'

He rubbed his brow. 'Just give me a few more weeks. Then I'll sort something out.'

'You'll tell her?'

'Yes, I'll have a discussion with her.'

Vanessa had heard this before. She gave him a kiss. Then she leaned back a little and adjusted his cravat. 'There,' she said. 'That's better.'

Unknown to Cecil, she'd dabbed a little bit of lipstick onto her finger and rubbed it beneath his collar.

She was tired of waiting. So she had a plan of her own to move things along.

Chapter Thirty-Seven

Philip and Augusta sat at a small table by a window in a tea room on Holloway Road. Through the pattern of the lace curtain, Augusta could see it was almost dark outside.

Searching through the old files had left them in a sombre mood.

'I knew there was a reason I tried to forget the war,' Philip said at last, his voice low. He looked down at his tea as he slowly stirred it. 'Revisiting those times brings back nothing but painful memories. I've done my best not to think about it these past four years. I thought... I thought the worst of it was behind me. That I'd finally got control of it. The memories.' He rubbed a hand over his eyes. 'But it keeps coming back, doesn't it, Augusta? Just when you think you've mastered the involuntary recollections—the ones that creep up in the middle of the night, clawing you out of sleep, heart pounding as if the war's still on. Just when you think you've silenced them for good—something like this drags it all back again. As if no time has passed at all.'

Augusta rarely saw him like this. She reached out and

took his hand, hoping the gesture would offer a little comfort. The visit to the railway arch had shaken Philip deeply.

'I'm not sure we'll ever be free of it,' she said gently. 'And maybe that's because we've spent so much time trying to forget. Maybe it isn't possible. Maybe we aren't meant to forget. The past is part of who we are now. It lives with us whether we like it or not.'

Philip shook his head. 'But I can't accept it, Augusta. I can't accept why I'm still here and so many good people are not. Why did Blake, Lennox, and Cavendish have to—' His voice faltered. 'They were better people than me. Braver. And yet here I am.'

Augusta felt a familiar lump rising in her throat. 'It wasn't about being deserving, Philip. You know that. It was luck. That's all it ever was. We made decisions. We followed orders. And when the time came, fate played its hand.'

He let out a long breath.

'I know exactly how you feel,' she continued. 'If it's any consolation, you're not alone. I carry the same weight. And there are others, too, living quiet lives, carrying their ghosts. We're all still here because… well, because we just are. There's no sense to it.'

Philip gave a weary nod and rubbed the back of his neck. 'We did what we could. We followed the code. We honoured the people we worked with. We survived. And Hastings… we trusted him.'

'We had to,' Augusta replied. 'We had to trust that everyone shared the same principles. That they'd put the mission—and each other—before themselves. But fear makes people do terrible things. And there are always some who will sacrifice others if it means saving themselves.'

She noticed Philip's jaw tighten. 'And Hastings'

betrayal caught up with him in the end,' he said. 'Someone poisoned him. We know that now. The question is—was it connected to what happened in Belgium? Or does this all come down to the painting and that rediscovered artist?' His gaze darkened. 'And forgive me, Augusta, because I know this sounds callous, but after what I've learned looking at those files… when I find Hastings' murderer—I might just have to shake their hand.'

Augusta said nothing for a moment. She didn't approve of the sentiment—but she couldn't entirely disagree either. 'We'll find the truth, Philip,' she said at last. 'Whatever Hastings was... he was once one of us. We need to understand how it came to this.'

Philip gave a slow nod. 'Let's finish what we started.'

Chapter Thirty-Eight

HARRIET CALLED on Fred at the bookshop the following day. Augusta felt happy watching them together, especially when Fred proudly showed Harriet the books he'd repaired. The pair had been courting for a few months now and Augusta felt encouraged that their fondness for each other showed no sign of diminishing.

Augusta spent the morning tidying shelves and rearranging some of the displays. She enjoyed making her shop look welcoming to customers, she'd recently bought some more chairs for people to sit and read in. As she worked, she was reminded how happy she felt in her shop. After the sombre revelations the previous day, she realised how important it was to appreciate what she had and enjoy it. Although she couldn't escape the past, she could make the most of life now and feel hopeful for the future.

A future with Philip? It was what she wanted but now was not the right time to discuss their plans. He was working quietly in his office upstairs, alone with his thoughts. She decided to leave him that way for the time being. He would come and find her again when he was ready.

The bell on the door sounded and Augusta turned to see Lady Hereford arriving in her bath chair. She was accompanied by her nurse and a white-haired lady carrying a little Pomeranian dog.

Augusta couldn't resist a smile. It looked like Lady Hereford and the Dowager Lady Pontypool were now friends.

'There he is!' said Lady Hereford pointing at Sparky's cage on the counter. 'Wheel me over to him Doris.'

The nurse did so, giving Augusta a cursory greeting as she passed. Lady Hereford and her new friend were too preoccupied with Sparky to notice her.

'He's your budgerigar?' asked Lady Pontypool.

'Canary!'

'Oh sorry, canary. Of course he is. He's a lovely shade of yellow, isn't he?'

The two ladies peered in at the little bird in his cage.

'Shall I fetch the bird seed?' asked Augusta joining them at the counter.

'Yes please,' said Lady Hereford. 'And hello Augusta! This is the Dowager Lady Pontypool. I've come to show her your shop and she's also here to meet Sparky.'

'How lovely to meet you, Augusta,' said Lady Pontypool. 'I've heard all about you.'

'Have you?' Augusta picked up the bag of bird seed, wondering what Lady Hereford had told her.

'Oh yes. I've heard how clever you are repairing books and selling them again. This really is a delightful shop.' She glanced around.

'Thank you,' said Augusta, handing her the bag of bird seed.

'Oh I won't feed him,' said Lady Pontypool passing the bag to her friend. 'I don't want my fingers pecked.'

'He doesn't peck fingers,' said Lady Hereford. 'He's very gentle. Watch.'

Lady Pontypool received a lesson on how to feed bird seed to a canary then Fred and Harriet were introduced to her after they came out of the workshop. Augusta made some tea.

'Is Sparky allowed out for a little fly?' asked Lady Pontypool as they drank their tea.

'No not in the shop,' said Lady Hereford.

'But doesn't he get bored in his little cage?'

'I let him fly around my flat,' said Augusta.

'But what about flying around the shop?' said the Dowager Lady Pontypool.

'I think he would love to fly around the shop,' said Lady Hereford. 'But Augusta has strict rules about these things.'

'I don't have any strict rules,' said Augusta, keen to show she wasn't a strict person.

'Then let him have a fly around the shop,' said Lady Pontypool with a glint in her eye. 'I'm sure he'd like it.'

'He'd love to,' said Lady Hereford.

'I want to see him fly,' said her friend.

'He's very good at it,' responded Lady Hereford.

Augusta gave in and opened the little door in Sparky's cage. Everyone watched as he cocked his head to one side, intrigued by the open door. Then he took off with a little flutter and swooped over to a bookcase by the stairs.

Lady Pontypool gave a whoop of delight and clapped her hands. 'There he goes!'

Lady Hereford grinned proudly.

Then Sparky took off again and landed on a bookcase

near the window. Lady Pontypool threw back her head and laughed.

Then he returned to the counter. Fred gave him a seed. He ate it then flew off again to the staircase.

'Oh I could watch him all day!' laughed Lady Pontypool.

Augusta resumed her tidying duties then helped a lady who came in looking for a reference book on wildflowers. Once she'd bought her book, she stayed to watch Sparky flying around the shop and visiting the counter for seeds.

Before long, other customers arrived and stayed. By the time Philip descended the stairs, the shop was lively with chatter. Everyone laughed as Sparky flew low over Philip's head then landed on the balustrade of the stairs.

'Sparky's showing off,' Augusta explained once Philip had joined her.

'So I can see. And he has quite an audience, doesn't he?' Philip smiled and Augusta felt relieved to see him looking a little brighter.

'Would you like a cup of tea?' she asked him.

'Thank you, Augusta. I'd love one.'

Chapter Thirty-Nine

'WILL you be letting Sparky out of his cage again today, Augusta?' asked Fred the following morning.

'I'm afraid not,' she replied. 'Not after yesterday.'

It had taken over an hour and a lot of bird seed and chopped apple to tempt the canary back to his cage the previous evening.

Sparky pecked at his bars, as if expecting to be released.

'Oh dear,' said Augusta. 'We've set a precedent now. He wants to be able to fly around the shop and it's not practical. Especially when it's so difficult to catch him again. I should never have listened to the Dowager Lady Pontypool. I should have stood my ground.'

'It's nice she and Lady Hereford are friends now,' said Fred.

'Yes it is nice, I'm happy they're getting on well. Although there's something rather mischievous about Lady Pontypool. I hope Lady Hereford stands up to her when need be.'

Fred smiled. 'I can't imagine them getting up to too much trouble.'

Augusta shook her head. 'You never know, Fred. Don't underestimate someone just because they're old.'

Sparky sat on his perch looking dejected. Augusta tried to cheer him up with some bird seed but he refused to take it from her.

Meanwhile, Fred leafed through the morning paper on the counter.

'Oh, look at this,' he said. 'There's been a theft from the National Gallery.'

Augusta joined him. 'Really?' she asked, leaning in. 'Is it the Veridiano painting?'

Fred shook his head. 'No—it's a Titian. *Venus and Adonis*. It says here it was taken from a storeroom.'

Augusta peered over his shoulder, reading the bold headline. 'Strange,' she said. 'For a moment I thought it might be the painting which vanished from Edward Galloway's office.'

'Edward Galloway?' said Fred. 'He was the gentleman who died suddenly at the National Gallery wasn't he?'

'That's right.'

Fred raised an eyebrow, he was clearly wondering how she knew a painting had gone missing from Galloway's office.

She lowered her voice to a whisper. 'I think you're close to guessing it, so I'll confirm it. Philip and I are working undercover on the case. Galloway was poisoned. But it's a secret investigation and I'm not allowed to talk about it.'

'Then there's no need to say anymore,' said Fred. 'I don't want to put you in a difficult position. And I know now why you wanted to look at Lillian Galloway's poetry.'

Augusta smiled. 'Yes. It seems she didn't have the best relationship with her father. I suppose she's a suspect but so are many other people. There's a lot to this case. And now we have another missing painting.' She frowned as she thought. 'How would anyone have known the Titian was in storage—unless they were tipped off?'

'Perhaps they just took an opportunity,' said Fred. 'They wandered into the storeroom and took the nicest picture they could find.'

'But they'd never get away with it framed,' said Augusta. 'They must have removed the canvas, rolled it up and hidden it under their overcoat. Audacious and also rather odd. I don't see how a thief could have got into that storeroom. Presumably it was locked?' She sighed. 'There's something very strange going on at the National Gallery. I'm going to speak to Philip about this.'

'A stolen Titian?' said Philip once Augusta had told him the news. 'Shall we go to the National Gallery and see if we can find out more?'

'As Mr and Mrs Parker?'

'I'm afraid so. I think it needs to be done. Let's see if Georgina Miller can tell us more.'

Chapter Forty

A SHORT WHILE LATER, they called at the secretaries' office at the National Gallery. Georgina Miller looked up from her typewriter, a slight frown creasing her brow, as Augusta and Philip stepped into the room. She stood, smoothing her black skirt.

'Mr and Mrs Parker,' she said. 'This is a surprise.'

Augusta offered a polite smile. She could hardly blame Miss Miller for being startled. Their presence here must seem peculiar. After all, what business did Edward Galloway's old friend have in a case of art theft?

'I know it's rather out of the blue,' Philip said. 'We're hoping to learn a little more about the recent theft. Edward would have been devastated to hear of it.'

'Yes, of course,' said Miss Miller. 'It's been quite a blow for the gallery. Everyone's in shock.'

'How did the thief manage it?'

'The police believe they picked the lock,' she said. 'And they also think the thief—or thieves—must have visited the gallery a few times beforehand. And somehow they found their way to the storeroom without raising suspicion.' She shook her head. 'It's unnerving to think someone was inside the gallery, preparing to steal from us. And the painting that was taken, *Venus and Adonis*, is very valuable. I don't know how they think they'll sell it. No one will touch it.'

'They might try the black market,' Augusta said quietly.

'I suppose,' Miss Miller agreed. 'But even there, it would raise eyebrows. It's far too well known.'

Philip shifted from one foot to another. Augusta sensed he was restraining himself from asking a barrage of questions. This sort of crime was familiar territory to him, precisely the type of case he'd have investigated during his days at Scotland Yard.

'Have the police made any progress?' he asked.

'Not much,' Miss Miller said with a sigh. 'They've been interviewing us all, asking if anyone saw anything out of the ordinary. But I haven't, and no one else has either. The police said it could be the work of a gang which they're already watching.'

'Well, I hope they're caught,' said Philip. 'Edward had a deep admiration for Titian. He'd be furious.'

Miss Miller gave a solemn nod. 'He would indeed.' She hesitated, then added, 'Actually, something rather unexpected happened during the search for the Titian.'

'Oh?'

'We found another painting,' said Miss Miller. '*Portrait of a Widow with a Lark*. The painting which had been in Mr Galloway's office. We thought it had already left for Italy.'

Augusta's heart gave a small jolt. 'Really? I thought it was on its way to a gallery in Florence.'

'It turned out it never left, it was here in the gallery all the time!'

Philip frowned. 'Where was it found?'

'It was in the storeroom all along. Rolled up and placed on top of one of the shelving units. One of the curators found it while we were all frantically searching for the Titian. At first, we thought it might be the missing work, but once they unrolled it, they realised what it was.'

'It had been removed from its frame?' Augusta asked.

Miss Miller nodded. 'Yes. And no label, no note, no explanation. Just tucked up there out of sight. We still don't know who put it there.'

'How strange,' said Philip. 'And where is it now?'

'Mr White-Thomas has it. He was delighted when it turned up.'

'I expect he was,' said Philip, scratching the back of his neck. 'Well,' he added, 'thank you, Miss Miller. You've been very helpful.'

They stepped out into the corridor once more, their footsteps echoing faintly against the polished floor.

Philip waited until they were alone before speaking. 'Someone took *Portrait of a Widow with a Lark* from Galloway's office and hid it,' he said. 'But why? Why hide it in the storeroom, and why not tell anyone?'

Augusta shook her head. 'I don't know. But it wasn't a mistake. You don't roll up a painting like that and forget where you've put it.'

'No,' Philip said, his voice low. 'You hide it because you don't want anyone to know it's still here.'

'I'd like to speak to Mr White-Thomas about it,' said Philip as they left the gallery. 'But we annoyed him last time, didn't we? I doubt we'd get much out of him now, especially if we go in under false pretences again.'

'He'd see through us in an instant,' Augusta said.

'If only this were a proper investigation,' Philip

muttered. 'We could ask lots of questions. At least the police are involved now with the stolen Titian. That gives me hope. I think I'll find out who's assigned to the case and see what they've uncovered. It would be interesting to know if anyone else is sensing something strange behind the scenes here at the gallery.'

'But you can't tell them what we've been assigned to do,' Augusta warned. 'Not unless Wetherell gives us permission.'

'Wetherell is a nuisance,' Philip said with a scowl.

'He led us to the railway arch,' Augusta reminded him.

Philip sighed. 'That's true. And we didn't really finish looking, did we? Not properly.'

'No. And I wouldn't blame you if you didn't want to go back. It wasn't easy.'

Philip gave a small nod. 'No, it wasn't. But we left too much unexplored. If there's a chance of uncovering more, I think we have to go back.' He paused for a moment, then added, 'But first, I want to know who hid *Portrait of a Widow with a Lark*. Someone deliberately removed it from its frame and stashed it in that storeroom.'

'And whoever it was,' said Augusta, 'wasn't very good at hiding it. The top of a shelf isn't exactly secure.'

'No, but it was out of sight. Maybe that was all they needed. Just enough to delay discovery. To keep it off the record until they were ready to move it.'

They stepped out into the bustle of Trafalgar Square. The wind had picked up, and a cluster of children shrieked with laughter as they tossed crusts of bread toward a flurry of eager pigeons. A newspaper seller shouted headlines nearby, his voice hoarse and insistent.

'Did you hear that?' Philip said suddenly.

'Hear what?' Augusta had been dwelling on the case rather than paying attention to her surroundings.

'The newspaper seller. He mentioned a robbery at an antique shop.'

Augusta frowned. 'That's awful.'

'It made me think of Owen Ridley.'

'Ridley doesn't have an antique shop,' she said. 'He calls it an antiquaries shop which is different, I think. Although frankly, it's more of a junk shop.'

Philip didn't reply. He was already striding towards the newspaper seller. Moments later, he returned with a folded newspaper in hand. He pulled out his reading glasses and examined it.

'I knew it,' he said, pointing at the front page. 'A robbery at Ridley's Antiquaries and Curios just off Tottenham Court Road. The article says the owner was attacked.'

Augusta stared at him. 'Owen Ridley was attacked?'

She watched Philip read the short report, his face serious.

'He's in hospital. It doesn't give details, but it sounds serious.'

'That's dreadful,' said Augusta. 'Maybe he tried to fight off the thieves. Or... perhaps it wasn't just a robbery.'

Philip looked up. 'You think it's connected?'

'He found Veridiano's sketchbooks. He knew Edward Galloway. And now he's been attacked,' said Augusta. 'That doesn't feel like a coincidence to me.'

'No,' Philip said. 'It doesn't.'

He folded the newspaper, but his thoughts were clearly still racing.

'If this is connected to Galloway's death,' Augusta said, 'then Ridley might have been a threat to someone.'

'Or he knew something he wasn't supposed to,' Philip replied.

Chapter Forty-One

PHILIP WENT to his office when they returned to the bookshop. He returned moments later with a piece of paper in his hand and showed it to Augusta.

'Have a look at this,' he said. Augusta read the message.

If you want to find out what happened to Venus and Adonis, *call at this address tomorrow at two o'clock: 4 Grand Union Buildings, George Street, EC2.*

Augusta frowned. 'Who sent this?'

'I've no idea at all. No name, no signature.'

'What about the postmark?'

'There wasn't one. It was hand-delivered. Someone must have pushed it through my letterbox while we were out.'

Augusta felt a slow chill creep up her spine. 'I don't like the fact someone knows where to find us. Do you think someone at the National Gallery discovered our real identities?'

'But this can't be from anyone there,' said Philip. 'It has to be from the person who stole the Titian painting.'

'Maybe it isn't, maybe it's someone pretending they know where the Titian is.' She handed the message back to Philip. 'Should we tell the police?'

'Not yet. I don't want to compromise our investigation.'

'It's tempting to think the message is from Wetherell, but it's not really his style of doing things.'

'No. Wetherell likes to be a little more obscure in his methods. But let's look on the bright side. What if this message is from someone trying to help us? It could be someone who has information they're too frightened to share openly.'

The thought was reassuring. 'I suppose you could be right.'

'We'll know soon enough,' said Philip. 'Tomorrow, in fact. In the meantime, I'm going to pay a visit to Scotland Yard and see what I can find out about the stolen Titian and the attack on Owen Ridley. I'll report back.'

Chapter Forty-Two

VANESSA CURWEN's voice trembled with fury as she asked the switchboard operator to put her through to Cecil White-Thomas at the National Gallery.

The call went through to his secretary, but it wasn't long before she heard his clipped, familiar tone.

'White-Thomas speaking.'

'You fool,' Vanessa hissed. 'You absolute fool.'

A pause followed before he spoke. 'What on earth are you talking about, Vanessa?'

'Don't play games,' she snapped. '*Portrait of a Widow with a Lark*. I spoke to one of the curators earlier who told me it had been found. You hid it in a storeroom. That was your idea of a secure hiding place?'

He lowered his voice—so low she could barely hear. 'I was planning to hide it more securely,' he said. 'But I didn't have much time when I retrieved it from Galloway's office. I thought it was out of sight, hidden on top of the shelving. Who was going to search up there? How was I supposed to know the hunt for *Venus and Adonis* would lead someone straight to it?'

'You should have moved it,' she hissed. 'Now it looks even more suspicious.'

'It was going to resurface eventually, remember? We had our excuse ready. Trouble with transport and a delay getting it to Italy. That's what we agreed.'

'Oh please, Cecil. No one's going to believe that now. There was no transport issue. You just rolled it up and dumped it on a shelf. You should have put it in secure storage like you've done with the Titian.'

'Ah yes, the luxury of hindsight, Vanessa. Do try to remember the difficulty I had removing it from Galloway's office undetected. I had minutes. There was no time to get clever with hiding places. But listen, no one's linking it to us. The gallery's relieved the Veridiano's still here and everyone's focused on the missing Titian. And that's going exactly to plan. Soon Mr Fisher and Mrs Peel will be the ones in trouble, and we'll be left to get on with our real work, uninterrupted.'

He was trying to soothe her, but she wasn't convinced. Her chest tightened with fury. He'd made a mess of this and he couldn't even admit it. If he bungled something so simple, what else might he ruin?

'This is amateur behaviour, Cecil. And you know as well as I do that we can't afford to be amateurs.'

'It's a minor inconvenience,' he said. 'It doesn't jeopardise the bigger plan.'

'It had better not. And if anyone so much as suspects I had the slightest involvement… don't think I won't name you first, Cecil.'

'That's rather uncalled for! And I don't appreciate being telephoned while you're in this kind of mood. When you next speak to me, make sure you've calmed down.'

She opened her mouth to respond, but the line had already gone dead.

Chapter Forty-Three

CECIL WAS late home that evening. He'd been working hard on the last-minute arrangements to frame Philip Fisher and Augusta Peel. Tomorrow they would be arrested! He couldn't wait.

He smiled to himself as he lifted the silver cloche from the plate left on the sideboard. Steam no longer rose from the dish. The chicken, congealed in its sauce, looked unappealing but he was too hungry to care. He carried it to the table, tucked a serviette into his collar, and picked up his knife and fork.

Margaret breezed into the dining room, her heels clicking smartly on the floor. She rested a hand on the back of the chair opposite him.

'Why are you so late, Cecil?'

He didn't look up. 'I'll explain after I've eaten.'

'No. You'll explain now.'

He set his cutlery down with a sharp clatter and glared at her.

'Must we do this immediately? I've had a busy day.'

'You're always having busy days. I'm tired of the

secrets, Cecil. You come and go like a shadow. You tell me nothing.'

He exhaled slowly through his nose. 'There's nothing to tell you about today Margaret. It was just another day of detailed academic research on Giovanni di Luca Veridiano.'

'Oh him. I'm tired of hearing about him. Sometimes I think he's all you ever talk about.'

He sat back in his chair, incredulous. 'You do realise I've happened across one of the most exciting discoveries of the twentieth century, Margaret? A talented Renaissance artist who was forgotten about for four hundred years!'

'So you keep telling me.'

'The history of art will need to be rewritten!'

Her expression remained impassive.

He sighed. Margaret had no appreciation of these things. She had little interest in the arts and he couldn't understand it.

'The housekeeper collected our laundry earlier today,' she said.

'Did she?' He resumed his meal. 'Three cheers for the housekeeper.' He couldn't understand why Margaret would bore him with something so mundane.

'The housekeeper told me they couldn't get one of your collars completely clean.'

'I see.' He put a mouthful of chicken in his mouth, wondering when his wife was going to leave him in peace.

'It had bright red lipstick on it,' she added.

Cecil choked on his chicken. 'What?'

'On the underside of the collar. They tried to clean it but there's still a stain. I don't know how it got there. I don't own any lipstick that red. Do you know how it got there, Cecil?'

'Of course not,' he replied once he'd gulped down his mouthful. The lump felt painful in his throat. 'Sometimes someone else's laundry gets muddled up with ours doesn't it? What was it that happened with my socks that time? Did they go missing? Or did we receive extra pairs? I can't remember but they do get muddled up there.'

'It's your collar, Cecil. Stop trying to come up with excuses.'

Silently he cursed Vanessa. Somehow she'd got her lipstick on his collar. When? Had she planned it? Or had she just been careless?

He let out a dry laugh. 'Very peculiar. I don't know how it got there.'

'No? Still not going to admit it?'

'Admit what? That lipstick somehow got on my collar? Perhaps it wasn't lipstick, maybe it was something else. Raspberry juice perhaps.'

'It's her lipstick, isn't it?' Her voice was quiet now. Icy. 'The woman you're having an affair with.'

She'd worked it out. Cecil never imagined she would.

He had to act outraged. He dropped his cutlery onto his plate, pulled the serviette from his collar and tossed it onto the table.

'I beg your pardon, Margaret. That's a disgusting accusation!'

'I've suspected for months.'

Her face was impassive now. Cold. Controlled.

'I'm leaving you,' she said.

He jumped to his feet, knocking his thighs against the table. 'Leaving me? Don't be ridiculous. Where would you go?'

'To my sister's.'

She turned on her heel and walked out of the dining room.

His head span and his breaths came quick and fast. She was leaving? Now? He leaned against the table, steadying himself.

'Margaret!' he called out. 'Don't go! Come back! We need to discuss this properly!'

His words were met with silence.

Chapter Forty-Four

FLAKES of icy snow fell from the sky the following afternoon as Augusta and Philip made the short walk from Liverpool Street railway station to George Street.

'I spoke to Detective Inspector Graham at the Yard this morning,' said Philip. 'He's investigating the stolen Titian and they have no idea yet who could be behind the theft. There's a gang they suspected to begin with but all the members have alibis for the time of the theft. So it could be someone unknown to them or it might be an inside job.'

'A member of staff at the gallery who knew where the Titian was being stored?' asked Augusta.

Philip nodded. 'I really wanted to tell Graham about the anonymous letter inviting us here,' he continued. 'But I kept quiet about it for now. It will be interesting to see what happens at this meeting.'

'Did Inspector Graham tell you how Owen Ridley is doing?'

'Yes, he's making a good recovery apparently. It sounds like a nasty attack. Three masked men entered his shop shortly before closing time and demanded the money from the till. When Ridley refused, they hit him with an iron bar.'

Augusta winced. 'How awful!'

'After that, they emptied his till and fled. Poor chap.'

'Do you think it could be connected to Galloway's murder?'

'It sounds like a straightforward violent robbery to me. But it's possible it was an attempt on Ridley's life disguised as a robbery. I can't imagine the three men poisoning Galloway in the gallery. The security guards would have noticed them, I'm sure. But it's possible the poisoner hired three men to stage the robbery at Ridley's shop.'

'I think we should assume the attack is linked to the murder for now,' said Augusta. 'And with a bit of luck, Inspector Graham can help find out who was behind it.'

As they neared George Street, she felt an uneasy sensation in the pit of her stomach. 'I don't think we should go directly to the address to begin with,' she said. 'I think we should observe it from a distance and see who turns up first.'

'Alright,' said Philip. 'Let's get there and see what the situation is.'

George Street was a small, short thoroughfare which linked Great Eastern Street with Shoreditch High Street. A railway viaduct ran past its eastern end.

A delivery van passed them, then someone pushing a handcart. The warehouses of C White Removals and Storage occupied the northern section of the street. They glanced at the large warehouse building as they passed it.

'It looks respectable enough,' said Philip. 'The company seems an established firm.' He checked his watch. 'It's a few minutes before two o'clock. Shall we wait here?'

'Let's find a vantage point nearby,' said Augusta, feeling tense. 'Somewhere we can't be easily seen.'

They walked to the end of the short street and lingered beneath the dingy railway bridge. A group of workmen passed by, chatting and joking.

A few vehicles drove past and there were a few passers-by. But it was a quiet street with very little happening.

Philip checked his watch again. 'It's five past two,' he said. 'They must be waiting for us.' He moved as if preparing to walk to the warehouse.

Augusta felt a stab of alarm and grabbed his arm. 'No,' she said sharply. 'Something doesn't feel right.'

He turned to her, eyes narrowing. 'What doesn't?'

'It's too easy,' she whispered. 'Everything until now has been shrouded in secrecy and silence. Every clue we've chased has taken work. And then you receive an anonymous note telling you someone wants to explain the painting's disappearance? It doesn't fit…. This feels like bait.'

Philip's brow furrowed. 'A trap?'

Before Augusta could answer, movement at the far end of the street caught her eye. She tensed. 'Look.'

A group of men was advancing from Shoreditch High Street. At first glance, they could have been workmen, but their pace was too purposeful, their formation too tight. Augusta took a step back, drawing Philip with her into the deeper gloom of the viaduct's arch.

'Good grief,' said Philip. 'Police.'

There were two officers in plain clothes and four uniformed constables.

'Why are there so many of them?' said Philip. 'Just a moment… one of them is Inspector Graham!'

They watched as the officers walked up to the doors of the warehouse and knocked. The door was opened, and the men went in.

'I think we should go,' said Augusta, her hands trembling a little. 'The police clearly know something.'

'Yes, I think it's a good idea to leave,' said Philip. 'I don't want to encounter Graham and try to explain what we're doing here.'

'This isn't a coincidence,' she said. 'Someone has tipped them off. Either about the painting—or about us.'

Philip nodded grimly. They turned and slipped away.

Chapter Forty-Five

It didn't take Detective Inspector Graham long to track Augusta and Philip down. Two hours later he sat with them in Philip's office.

He was a broad-shouldered man with a greying moustache and sharp blue eyes. 'We received an anonymous tip-off yesterday afternoon,' he said. 'A report that the Titian stolen from the National Gallery was being held at the C White depository in George Street.'

'Really?' said Augusta. She thought it best to feign ignorance at this stage.

'When we entered the premises, we found the painting rolled up and carefully packed inside a box,' continued Graham. 'It had been deposited in a secure locker two days' previously.'

'So you've found the missing painting?' said Philip.

Graham gave a firm nod. 'Absolutely. I've no idea who tipped us off. However....' He paused and fixed them with his gaze. 'The gentleman who deposited the painting gave his name as Philip Fisher.'

Augusta startled. Who'd done such a thing?

Philip shook his head. 'Someone's trying to frame me.'

It had been a trap after all.

The inspector watched them both, his expression unreadable. Would he believe Philip?

'I'm inclined to take you at your word, Fisher,' he said eventually. 'If someone was depositing a stolen painting at a secure storage facility, he wouldn't use his real name.'

'Exactly,' Augusta said. 'Whoever did this wants the blame to fall on Philip.'

Graham gave a thoughtful nod, folding his hands in front of him. 'My colleagues at the Yard speak highly of you, Fisher. By all accounts, you left the Yard with your integrity intact. So that leaves me with one very troubling question—why would someone go to the effort of setting you up? And what, precisely, are you investigating that might make someone want to discredit you?'

A pause followed. Philip exchanged a glance with Augusta. Should they tell Inspector Graham the truth?

Augusta's thoughts raced. Their orders from Wetherell had been clear: no official interference, just as it had been during the war. If Scotland Yard learned Edward Galloway had been murdered, they'd take over the investigation.

She tried to communicate all this to Philip in a single glance. He turned to the inspector and said, 'Mrs Peel and I have been working undercover at the National Gallery where the Titian was supposedly stolen from.'

For a dreadful moment, Augusta thought he was going to tell Graham everything. Her breath caught. If Philip chose to speak freely, there'd be no way to stop him now.

He continued, calmly, 'We've been tasked with locating a missing painting.'

Augusta exhaled, slowly. He was improvising a cover story.

'It's a piece by a recently rediscovered Renaissance artist, Veridiano,' Philip went on. '*Portrait of a Widow with a Lark*. It disappeared from a private office at the National Gallery.'

The inspector folded his arms. 'And how does that relate to the Titian which was stolen?'

'The stolen Titian must have been a set-up. Someone learned who we really are and didn't like us asking questions about the Veridiano. They hid the Titian at the warehouse and used my name. I believe this was orchestrated to discredit me before Mrs Peel and I got too close to the truth.'

Inspector Graham studied him in silence, then nodded slowly. 'So you're telling me the Titian wasn't actually stolen?'

'I don't believe so.'

Graham tutted. 'They're wasting police time. Dragging my officers out on a false trail.'

'Precisely,' said Philip. 'But I intend to find out who's behind this. And once I do, I'll tell you right away, Graham.'

The inspector nodded. 'Thank you, Fisher. I'm satisfied with your explanation. Please keep me informed.'

'You have my word,' said Philip.

The two men shook hands and Augusta felt a welcome sense of relief. Graham believed them and they hadn't compromised their investigation.

'So what do you think?' Philip asked Augusta once Graham had left.

'I think you summarised it perfectly just now,' she said. 'Someone is trying to discredit you. And it has to be someone at the National Gallery. They had access to the

Titian and they've somehow worked out who we really are.'

Philip nodded. 'It seems Mr and Mrs Parker weren't very convincing after all. But never mind, I feel we're managing to narrow down our suspects now. Cecil White-Thomas. Is it possible he's discovered our true identities? I never did warm to him. We need to investigate him further. But how?'

'We need evidence he's been up to no good,' said Augusta. 'And to find evidence, we need to have a good look around his office.'

Philip's eyes widened. 'We break in during the night?'

Augusta nodded. 'That's exactly what we do. Tonight.'

The thought was unnerving. But Augusta wanted to find the evidence before Cecil White-Thomas hid it.

Chapter Forty-Six

Augusta and Philip got to the National Gallery shortly before closing time. They strolled through the galleries, pretending to admire the paintings.

A bell rang out, signalling it was time for everyone to leave.

'This way,' whispered Philip, walking in the opposite direction to the exit. A short corridor took them from the Flemish School gallery to the Late Venetian School. In the wall was a door marked "Private".

Philip glanced around to check no one was about, then pushed it open.

Augusta followed, holding her breath.

They stepped into a long, dimly lit corridor lined with plain doors. Augusta's heart pounded. If anyone appeared now, she and Philip would be seen and challenged. 'We need somewhere to hide,' she whispered.

Philip nodded. 'Let's go.'

She followed him, trying to keep her footsteps as quiet as possible. They reached a set of double doors. Philip cautiously pushed against one and peered through the gap. 'All clear,' he whispered.

They entered a corridor with a corner at the end.

Augusta prayed no one would come marching around the corner and see them.

They continued on their way, trying to move quickly yet quietly. Augusta knew it wouldn't be easy for Philip with his walking stick.

Then she heard a door slam. Followed by footsteps.

Her heart leapt into her mouth. 'Someone's coming!' she hissed.

Philip halted. Then he turned to the door next to them and gave it a gentle push.

It was locked. 'Oh dear,' he said.

The footsteps were growing louder, approaching the corner ahead of them. Augusta turned, heading back for the double doors. She heard Philip follow behind her.

She pushed against another door, but it was also locked. Even if they did find a door which opened, it was possible there'd be someone in the room beyond it. Then they would have to explain themselves.

Just as they would have to explain themselves to the person rapidly approaching them now.

The mission felt doomed. How were they going to find the evidence Cecil White-Thomas was up to something?

'In here!' came a whisper behind her.

She spun round to see Philip holding open a door, she darted into the darkness beyond it and he followed.

Augusta couldn't go far, the room was tiny. In the moment before Philip closed the door behind them, she saw buckets, mops and brooms.

They were in a cleaning cupboard.

It wasn't long before the footsteps they'd heard strode past the cupboard. Augusta slowed her breathing. 'How long do you think we had before they found us? Ten seconds?'

'Something like that,' came Philip's voice from the darkness. 'This was a stroke of luck.'

'Unless a cleaner turns up.'

'Yes that's a possibility. But for now, we'll just have to wait. I'm sure this will be worth our while, Augusta.'

She sighed. 'I hope so.'

Chapter Forty-Seven

THERE WAS JUST enough space in the cupboard to turn over a couple of buckets and use them as seats. They'd come prepared for the wait. Augusta pulled her torch from her handbag and a pack of cards.

They played in silence for a while, the torchlight glinting off the face of the cards. Every creak in the distance made Augusta tense.

An hour later, the stillness of the gallery seemed to deepen. Philip opened the door a little and peered out.

'It's dark out here,' he whispered. 'All the lights are out. I think we should go now. Let's hope we don't meet any security guards on the way.'

They crept from their hiding place and cautiously made their way to Cecil White-Thomas's office. Augusta led the way with her torch, clasping her palm over the lens to keep the beam as subdued as possible. She winced at the noise their footsteps made.

Eventually they reached the corridor where the office was located. They hurried now, keen to get to the door.

When they got there, Philip pulled a skeleton key from

his pocket and fitted it into the lock. Augusta held her breath.

A click.

The door opened.

They slipped inside and locked the door behind them. Augusta exhaled slowly, but her nerves remained taut. 'If the guard's nearby, he might have heard that.' She pulled a spare torch from her handbag and handed it to Philip.

'We need to move quickly,' he said. He put on his reading glasses and stepped over to the desk.

Augusta swept her torch beam over the bookshelves and came across a filing cabinet. She crossed over to it and pulled out a drawer. The folders were meticulously arranged—the names of artists listed alphabetically.

She found V, then a file for Veridiano.

She tugged the folder free, pulse quickening, and brought it to the desk. As she opened the file, her torchlight fell on old yellowing documents and handwritten notes.

'Is this White-Thomas's handwriting?' she asked. 'Actually it can't be. These pages look old.' They were filled with a cramped script, written in Italian.

Philip leaned in, peering at the faded ink. 'These must be originals,' he said. 'Possibly from Veridiano himself.'

'Pages from his sketchbook?'

'They could be.'

Augusta carefully lifted the yellowed papers, revealing a stack of pale, pristine sheets beneath. She frowned, a little puzzled. 'Some blank paper,' she said. 'Perhaps it's here to protect the old papers.'

Then she found another old page. 'This has got a few lines written on it, but the sentence stops halfway through.'

'How do you know it isn't just a short note?'

'Because it stops mid-word,' Augusta replied. 'And the spelling of the previous word is wrong.'

'You're confident it's incorrect?'

'I know enough Italian to spot a mistake.' She continued looking through the papers, finding more incomplete pages. 'It's as if Veridiano was practising... Would he really have kept these papers in his sketchbooks?'

'It seems unlikely,' said Philip.

'And here's some old paper which is completely blank. It looks old and yet there's nothing on it.'

She picked up a sheet and examined it closely with her torch. Then, instinctively, she brought the paper to her nose.

Philip watched her, puzzled. 'You're sniffing the paper now?'

'It doesn't smell right,' she said quietly. 'Old paper has a scent. Dust, grease, sometimes mildew... a musty smell, perhaps. But for paper which is over four hundred years old, this just smells like... paper. New paper.' She rubbed her fingers on it. 'And there's another smell too. Very faint, but it's there. Tea.'

Philip let out a soft laugh. 'Tea? This paper has tea on it?'

Augusta nodded, feeling a satisfying sense of realisation. 'Tea has been used to make the paper look old. It's a known technique, isn't it? Tea to darken the paper and maybe some singeing at the edges to make it look time worn. Anyone with a little patience could do it. But it's not convincing when you look closely.'

'Well I never,' said Philip. 'So we're looking at some pages which White-Thomas has created to practise an aging technique. And once he perfected it, he must have made the sketchbooks.'

The rediscovered Renaissance artist wasn't real. 'Veridiano is White-Thomas's invention!' Augusta said. 'He created the legend and fabricated the material to support it!'

'So this means the rediscovered paintings could be forgeries,' said Philip. 'Have we uncovered an enormous ruse?'

Augusta grinned. 'I think we have.'

'So White-Thomas made the sketchbooks and Ridley found them in a cheap box of rubbish he bought at auction. Or so he says. Do you think he could be in on it?'

'I don't know,' said Augusta. 'It's possible he wasn't and was fooled by the sketchbooks. Perhaps he wanted to believe he'd found something genuinely valuable.'

'And he took the sketchbooks to the expert on Renaissance art, Cecil White-Thomas,' said Philip. 'He must have been overjoyed to receive them.'

'I bet he was,' said Augusta. 'His work had paid off. And White-Thomas's fraud is beginning to make sense now. Just a few months after Ridley found the sketchbooks, *The Melancholy of Saint Aurelia* was found during a house clearance in Hampstead after the supposed death of an elderly recluse. Was it a forged painting which had somehow been planted there?'

'I think so,' said Philip. 'Mr Sandford at *The Art Chronicle* told us the painting sold for a good sum of money at auction and Vanessa Curwen was involved with its sale. Could she be in on the fraud too?'

Augusta nodded. 'She could be.'

'There was another painting she mentioned, *Allegory of the Four Humours*,' said Philip. 'From what I remember, that turned up only recently too. I don't believe we know where, though.'

'Then there's *Portrait of a Widow with a Lark*,' said Augusta. 'Found in the vestry of a church in Croydon. I can't imagine it would have been too difficult to plant there. Three paintings by Veridiano suddenly surfaced here in London a short while after the sketchbooks were found by Ridley. Why have no paintings been found elsewhere? No one's mentioned any being found in Italy—not even in Veridiano's supposed birthplace of Florence. I'm only realising now how orchestrated this is!'

'So who painted them?' said Philip. 'White-Thomas?'

'I've never heard anyone suggest he has any artistic talent,' said Augusta. 'Not even casually. Maybe Galloway painted them?'

'Now there's a thought, he was certainly talented enough. You think Galloway could have been part of the fraud and fell out with Cecil-White?'

'It's possible.'

'Yes it is. Alternatively, another forger was used,' said Philip. 'And I don't think they'd be too difficult to find. The rediscovered artworks have fooled a lot of people and there aren't many forgers in London who are that good. I know an informant who might be able to help us with names.'

Augusta smiled. 'That would be wonderful! If we can find the forger, then White-Thomas has no defence whatsoever.'

'So what about Galloway?' said Philip. 'How does he fit into all of this? Was he in on the fraud too? Let's not forget *Portrait of a Widow with a Lark* was in his office when he was murdered.'

'We were told he was working on it,' said Augusta. 'Examining it.'

'He knew a lot about art,' said Philip. 'Perhaps he discovered the painting was a fake? He may have spotted the canvas or pigments were too modern.'

'Yes!' Augusta felt excited by this thought. 'He told White-Thomas and that was the last thing White-Thomas wanted to hear. It would have panicked him. If the forgery was exposed, his entire scheme would unravel.'

'So White-Thomas poisoned Galloway and took the painting,' said Philip. 'He wanted to hide it before anyone else examined it and realised it was forged.'

'And he falsified paperwork to show the painting was on its way to an exhibition in Florence,' said Augusta. 'At a fake art gallery.' She gave a laugh. 'Why didn't we realise this sooner?'

'We've realised it now,' said Philip. 'Let's see if we can find the forger. Then we can report back to Inspector Graham. In the meantime, let's hope he's found some evidence White-Thomas stole the Titian and hid it in the warehouse.'

Beyond the door, slow footsteps echoed in the corridor.

They turned off their torches and ducked down behind the desk.

The footsteps drew closer. Then stopped.

Right outside the office door.

Augusta could barely allow herself to breathe. Her heartbeat pounded in her ears. She could feel Philip crouching tense beside her, she knew his position would be hurting his leg.

Then the door handle turned. A pause followed, then came a rattle of the handle. Whoever was outside was trying to get in.

Augusta held her breath. Had someone heard them talking or noticed their torchlight? She thought they'd both been careful.

She squeezed her eyes shut as she heard a key slide into the lock.

The handle creaked then the door opened.

Augusta opened her eyes to see a torch beam spilling

into the room. She felt fearful that even the sound of air moving in her lungs might give them away.

Heavy-soled footsteps entered. Whoever it was paused just inside the door, surveying the room.

Augusta closed her eyes again and waited. Was the visitor a security guard checking the room? Or could it be Cecil White-Thomas?

She felt a prickle on the nape of her neck. If it was White-Thomas then he wouldn't let them leave. He'd already poisoned someone who'd discovered his secret. What would he do to her and Philip? It didn't bear thinking about.

A long moment of silence passed. The visitor took a few more steps, the torch sweeping the room like a search light.

Then the visitor left. The door closed behind them. The lock turned again.

'Good grief,' whispered Philip with a relieved sigh. 'That was close. We're going to have to wait here for a while until we can be sure the coast is clear.'

Chapter Forty-Eight

'WHAT'S THIS PLACE?' asked Augusta the following day. She and Philip stood outside a grimy-walled public house in Southwark. It was called The Black Pilchard and curtains covered the windows.

'Mr Hobb, the landlord, is very helpful,' said Philip, pushing open the door.

Inside, the dingy bar was low-ceilinged with dark woodwork. Sawdust covered the floor and the air was hazy with tobacco smoke.

'Mr Fisher!' said a man with crooked teeth behind the bar. He wore a collarless shirt and was polishing a tankard with a grubby rag. 'Not seen you in here for a while.'

Augusta had no idea Philip ever frequented places like this.

'Hello Hobb. This is my friend and colleague, Mrs Augusta Peel,' said Philip.

Mr Hobb beamed, revealing even more crooked teeth. 'A pleasure to meet you, Mrs Peel.' He turned back to Philip. 'What'll it be? Pint of the usual?'

'Thank you,' said Philip. 'Augusta?'

'I'll have a whisky and water, thank you.'

'Make yourselves comfortable over there,' said the landlord nodding to a booth with wooden partitioning. 'I'll bring the drinks over.'

They sat on the wooden benches at the table. Augusta glanced around and saw she was the only woman in the place. A thin man with a yellowing face gave them a sidelong glance as he shuffled past.

Mr Hobb joined them moments later.

'I hope you don't mind the sudden visit,' Philip said quietly. 'We're trying to find someone.'

'What sort of someone?' Hobb took a long sip from his tankard. 'Got a name?'

'No. But let's suppose I wanted a painting forged. I'd need someone talented and discreet.'

Mr Hobb gave him a long look. 'I hope this is part of an investigation and not a change in career, Fisher.'

'An investigation,' said Philip.

The landlord leaned back against the wooden partition which creaked from his weight. 'Well now... I can't say I deal with that crowd, Mr Fisher. Don't usually get that sort of element in here. But... strictly for argument's sake, I might know someone who knows someone.' He paused, glanced around, then leaned in. 'A friend of mine talks of someone called Harris. Works out of a garret studio on King Street, Covent Garden.'

Philip raised an eyebrow. 'Interesting'

'Quiet fellow. Doesn't advertise, if you catch my meaning. Charges a lot of money. But my friend says he's the one to see if you want something that looks convincing.'

'Well,' said Philip, 'your friend has been very helpful.'

Mr Hobb chuckled. 'I'll pass that on.' He got to his feet. 'Enjoy your drinks.'

. . .

'Hobb is an informant?' asked Augusta once they'd left The Black Pilchard and walked down a cobbled street. The river was close by and Augusta guessed the tide was out because she could smell the dank odour of the mud flats.

'Yes he is,' said Philip.

'Why? What does he get out of it?'

'It's complicated. Sometimes informants are paid by the police and sometimes things they do are... overlooked in return for information.'

'So they're criminals who don't get prosecuted if they help the police.'

'Sometimes.'

'Hobb is a criminal?'

'No! Hobb's not a criminal.'

'He just knows criminals.'

'He knows a lot of people. I've known him ever since I was a constable and I trust him. If he says Harris is our man then I think he's probably right.'

Chapter Forty-Nine

KING STREET was a lively thoroughfare in Covent Garden, busy with carts and vans from the nearby market. After making some inquiries, Augusta and Philip finally found Mr Harris's studio on the top floor of a tall, narrow building which housed a draper's shop.

The stairs creaked as they climbed the narrow, twisting staircase. The faint odour of linseed oil mingled with the tang of turpentine as they reached the top floor.

'This must be it,' said Philip, pausing by a door with a glazed panel covered by yellowing newspaper. He rapped gently.

For a moment, nothing happened. Then they heard the scrape of a stool and the shuffle of feet. A bolt rattled, and the door opened a cautious inch. A dark eye appeared in the gap.

'Yes?'

'Mr Harris?' said Philip. 'We'd like a word, if we may.'

The door opened a little wider. The man behind it was thin and pale with a hunched frame and paint-spattered clothes. His hair was thinning at the front and reached his shoulders in greying tangled clumps. He looked to be in his forties, although it was hard to tell. His face was hollow and sickly.

'Who's asking?' He looked them both up and down.

'We were told you might help us understand some paintings,' said Augusta.

The artist regarded them both for a little longer, then opened the door fully. 'You'd better come in.'

The garret was cluttered and lit by a window which overlooked the rooftops. Canvases were stacked against the walls and palettes lay scattered about, covered in dried paint. Jars were filled with brushes and an easel stood in the centre of the room, a half-finished painting of a landscape resting on it.

Harris motioned for them to sit on a pair of mismatched stools.

'Have you heard of the artist Giovanni di Luca Veridiano?' Philip asked him.

Harris pursed his lips. 'I'm not saying anything.'

'Mrs Peel and I are private detectives and we believe Veridiano, a supposedly rediscovered Renaissance artist, never existed.'

'I'm not saying anything,' he repeated.

'Why not?'

'Because I'll get into trouble.'

'Because Cecil White-Thomas asked you to paint three paintings? *The Melancholy of Saint Aurelia, Allegory of the Four Humours* and *Portrait of a Widow with a Lark*.'

Harris shrugged.

Silence fell and Augusta wondered how they'd be able to get the information they needed. She thought of Philip's relationship with Hobb, a police informant. 'If we promise to keep your identity secret, Mr Harris,' she ventured, 'will you tell us about Cecil White-Thomas?'

The artist raised his eyebrows, as if interested in this arrangement. 'How do I know you'll keep my identity quiet?' he asked.

Philip got to his feet and held out his hand. 'We'll give you our word and we'll shake on it.'

Harris stared at them both for a moment, his eyes wide like a frightened animal's. 'Alright then.' He held out his hand with paint-stained fingernails. 'I trust you. I don't know why, but I do.'

After shaking hands with them both, he sank into a threadbare easy chair by the window. 'I fell out with White-Thomas,' he said. 'That's why I'm talking. If he'd been a decent man, I'd keep quiet.'

'What did you do for him?' Philip asked.

'The three paintings you mentioned and the preliminary sketches to go with them. White-Thomas gave me references, drawings to mimic. He told me what kind of paint to use and said the work was for a historical art exhibition. I believed him at first.'

'When did you stop believing him?' asked Philip.

'When *The Melancholy of Saint Aurelia* fetched a lot of money at auction. The press were talking about a lost Renaissance master called Veridiano and that's when I realised I'd helped invent him.'

'Did White-Thomas pay you well?' Philip asked.

'Not well enough when you consider all the glory he's been basking in.' He scratched his head. 'I asked him for more money but he refused. He told me I was paid fairly for my work. I was actually thinking of going to the police about it at one point, but then I worried I'd get into trouble for being involved.'

'But it seems you never knew you were involved with anything criminal,' said Philip.

'Not this time. But…' He gave a wry smile. 'There

have been other times I've painted things which really I shouldn't have... I suppose that's how White-Thomas got to find out about me.'

'Did you keep records of the work you did for him?' asked Augusta. 'Any sketches?'

Harris nodded. 'A few.' He got up and crossed to the corner of the room where he rummaged through a trunk. From inside, he pulled out a sketchbook. 'In here are my early ideas.'

He handed it to Augusta and she flicked through, immediately recognising the sketches for *Portrait of a Widow with a Lark*. 'This could be enough,' she said. 'Enough to prove forgery.'

'Why are you happy to admit to this?' Philip asked Harris.

'Because I don't like the way White-Thomas treated me,' he replied. 'If he gets caught for this then I'll be very happy about it.'

'Then let us take this,' said Augusta, holding up the sketchbook. 'It will help bring him to justice.'

Harris nodded. 'You can take it. But please don't tell anyone my name. I never knew what I was caught up in and I don't want anything more to do with it. I just want to forget about it now. If anyone comes here asking me more questions, I'll deny everything.'

Philip nodded. 'Thank you for your time, Mr Harris. We'll keep your name out of it.'

Chapter Fifty

CECIL WHITE-THOMAS FOLDED his arms and narrowed his eyes at Detective Inspector Graham. He hadn't been told the purpose of this meeting at Scotland Yard, but he had a good idea. Veridiano. The forgotten Renaissance painter. Even if the inspector suspected the whole thing was a fabrication, Cecil wasn't worried. Policemen rarely knew the first thing about art. That was why so much art crime went undetected: it was too clever for them.

The door opened and another man stepped inside, leaning heavily on a walking stick.

Cecil smirked. 'So, you're ready to admit you're not Roger Parker now?'

Philip Fisher nodded and took a seat beside his colleague. 'That's right. I'm a private detective. And I'm assisting Inspector Graham today.'

Cecil scowled. 'This should be interesting. What am I supposed to have done?'

'We'd like to ask you about the painter Veridiano,' said Graham. 'Quite the rediscovery, I gather?'

Cecil gave a smile. 'Indeed. One of the most thrilling

art finds of the twentieth century. His sketchbooks and paintings turned up unexpectedly. A revelation.'

Graham consulted his notes. 'The very same sketchbooks we found in your office this morning.'

Cecil's smile froze. 'In my office? Who authorised that?'

'The Director of the National Gallery,' said Graham coolly. 'We were granted access at six o'clock this morning.'

Cecil's heart began to pound. 'You had no right to do that without my consent.'

'On the contrary,' said Fisher. 'There was a very good reason we didn't ask you first. You'd have hidden the evidence.'

Cecil sat forward sharply. 'What evidence?'

'Evidence of forgery,' said Graham. 'We've had a preliminary look, and I'd be surprised if any of those documents stand up to scrutiny.'

'They're not forged!' Cecil barked. 'They've been authenticated!'

'By whom?' asked Graham.

'By me!' Cecil's voice rose. 'Do you even know who I am? I have studied at Oxford, published three volumes on Venetian masters, consulted for—'

'Precisely,' interrupted Graham. 'And with that impressive pedigree, who would dare question your word? That's what made the deception so effective, wasn't it?'

Cecil glared at the two men. 'This is outrageous. Do you honestly believe I would risk everything—my reputation, my position—for what? A little excitement?'

'You tell us,' said Fisher quietly. He opened the folder in front of him and took out a sketchbook. He opened it and the page displayed a sketch for *Portrait of a Widow with a Lark*.

So they'd found Harris. Cecil suppressed a curse word and rubbed at his jaw. His fingers brushed across the roughness of two-day-old stubble, he'd forgotten to shave since Margaret had left him.

'The artist claims you paid him to paint three works,' said Fisher.

Cecil shrugged. 'He's lying.'

Inspector Graham folded his arms. 'We don't think he's lying,' he said. 'This sketchbook supports his claims. And let's not forget all those forged papers we've found in your office. There's no getting out of this Mr White-Thomas.'

A chill ran through him. There had to be a way out.

'Sketches prove nothing,' he said. "They could have been made at any time. He might have copied the Veridiano paintings out of admiration. Artists do that.'

Fisher smiled faintly. 'Except Veridiano never existed. You forged the sketchbooks and ensured Owen Ridley found them. You made sure Veridiano's undiscovered works were found in old houses and churches where they'd supposedly been sitting for generations. And then Edward Galloway interrupted your plans.'

Cecil gave a laugh. 'Galloway?'

'He was the curator of provenance research at the National Gallery,' said Fisher. 'Like everyone else, he was intrigued by Veridiano's work. He asked to examine *Portrait of a Widow with a Lark*, didn't he? And what did he discover? He realised it was a fake.'

How had Fisher worked all this out? Cecil shook his head firmly. 'Not true.'

'You had to hide the painting, didn't you? You didn't want to risk anyone else discovering it was forged. That's why you falsified papers to show it had been sent to a gallery in Florence. A gallery which doesn't exist.'

Cecil gave a derisive sniff. 'Have you finished yet, Fisher?'

'Not yet. You hid the painting in a store room and you

didn't like it when Mrs Peel and I asked you about it. We were a nuisance to you, weren't we?'

Cecil smiled. 'Now that's the one thing you and I can agree on.'

'You wanted to be rid of us so you took a Titian painting from a store room, reported it as stolen, and hid it in a warehouse near Liverpool Street station. You then arranged for Inspector Graham and me to meet at that location at the same time so my colleague would suspect I was behind the theft. It was a clear attempt to frame me, wasn't it, Mr White-Thomas?'

Cecil met his gaze. 'I've no idea what you're talking about, Mr Fisher.'

'You know exactly what I'm talking about. But unfortunately for you, Inspector Graham wasn't fooled. He knows my character.' Philip shook his head. 'Such a clumsy idea.'

Cecil gritted his teeth. It had seemed like a good plan at the time. 'This is all a story, Fisher. You can't prove any of it.'

'We can and we will. But we haven't got to the most serious crime yet, have we?'

'And what's that?'

'Galloway's murder.'

The words felt like a punch. Murder? Cecil's jaw dropped. 'He wasn't murdered. He died from a heart attack.'

Inspector Graham now leaned forward. 'Galloway didn't die of a heart attack, Mr White-Thomas. He was poisoned. Cyanide. In his coffee.'

'Poisoned?' Cecil whispered.

'Yes,' said Graham. 'You worked late with him that evening and made him coffee. Then you put poison in it.'

'You're accusing me of murder?' Cecil could scarcely believe what he was hearing. 'But I didn't do it! And why did everyone say he died of a heart attack if he was poisoned? I don't understand! I'm innocent!'

'Tell us more about Owen Ridley,' said Fisher. 'The man who supposedly discovered Veridiano's sketchbooks. Did he realise they were fake? Did he challenge you too?'

'No!' protested Cecil.

'Is that why you hired some men to attack him?'

'Absolutely not!' He struck the table with his fist, keen to demonstrate his innocence.

Then he sat back again and pushed his spectacles up his nose.

He didn't like the sceptical glances both men were now giving him. What did he have to say to make them believe him?

He took in a slow breath. He had another card to play and now was his chance to use it.

Chapter Fifty-One

'You need to arrest Vanessa Curwen,' Cecil told Mr Fisher and Inspector Graham.

Fisher's brow creased. 'She murdered Edward Galloway?'

'I don't know. But all this Veridiano business. It was all Vanessa's idea.' He'd admitted the fraud now. Soon, everyone would find out and his career would be over. But he was going to make sure he dragged Vanessa down with him.

'Miss Curwen orchestrated the whole thing?' asked Graham.

'Yes,' replied Cecil. Vanessa had ended his marriage and now he was taking revenge. 'She put me up to it,' he continued. 'She said it would be a clever little project.'

'Why would you go along with that, Mr White-Thomas? A man of your standing?'

Cecil crossed his arms. 'Because she's Vanessa Curwen. Do you know how much influence she has in the art world? When she says jump, you jump.'

'But I'm not sure that fits with what we know about you,' said Fisher. 'You've built your reputation on your own authority. You don't strike me as the sort of man who follows instructions blindly.'

'She's different,' Cecil said. 'We've crossed paths for years. She knows how to get what she wants.'

Fisher's eyes narrowed. 'How well do you really know her?' he asked.

'Well enough,' Cecil snapped. 'We work in the same circles.'

'And do you always do what she tells you to?'

'No. But she said we could invent a forgotten painter— Veridiano. We'd create a legacy, make money, and no one would question it. Have you heard how much she made from selling one of the paintings? She's the one who profited most from this.'

'As did you,' Fisher pointed out. 'You gained recognition, headlines and admiration.'

Cecil sneered. 'Vanessa is the mastermind, not me. Bring her in. She'll try to pin it all on me, of course.'

Philip nodded slowly. 'You've barely mentioned her until now. Then, all of a sudden, she's the architect of the whole thing.'

'You want the truth? I'm giving it to you.'

'Or you're trying to save your own skin,' said Fisher. 'We'll speak to Miss Curwen. But if she denies your version of events, then it's merely your word against hers.'

'Just talk to her,' Cecil snapped. 'She'll twist it, of course. She always does. But she's the one you should be questioning. Not me. And as for Galloway's murder… that's nothing to do with me. I'm admitting everything else but I'm not a murderer. Perhaps Vanessa did it? Who knows. I wouldn't put it past her. I wasn't working late that evening with Galloway, I was at home with my wife! Just ask her and she'll tell you.'

Inspector Graham made some notes and Cecil felt a pang of worry as he wondered what Margaret would say when they asked her to provide an alibi for him. Would she comply?

Chapter Fifty-Two

VANESSA WAS busy rearranging a display of paintings when two men arrived at her gallery. She recognised one of them immediately. Mr Fisher the private detective. He was accompanied by a broad-shouldered man with a greying moustache and sharp blue eyes.

She wasn't pleased to see them. Fisher's accomplice looked suspiciously like a police detective. But she gave them both a wide, charming smile as they stepped in through the door.

'Mr Parker,' she said. 'This is a surprise.'

'I was working undercover when you met me previously. My name is Mr Fisher and I'm a private detective. But I suspect you knew that already.' He turned to his colleague. 'This is Detective Inspector Graham of Scotland Yard.'

The Yard. Vanessa felt her stomach knot.

'A private detective?' she said. 'I never would have guessed. Then let's speak somewhere more private, shall we?' She smoothed her hair and fluttered her eyelashes.

Graham seemed to appreciate this but Fisher was unmoved.

She walked over to her desk and the two men followed.

'What can you tell us about Giovanni di Luca Veridiano?' asked Fisher once they were seated.

It was clear they'd discovered something. But she didn't know what they knew, so she had to keep up the pretence. 'A rediscovered Renaissance artist,' she said cheerily.

'He's fictional,' said Graham.

Vanessa continued smiling. So they had found out. 'Is he?' she said as innocently as possible.

'Don't mess us about Miss Curwen,' said Graham. 'Mr White-Thomas has told us everything.'

'Has he?' This question came from genuine surprise. Why had Cecil confessed? She felt sure he would deny everything to the bitter end.

'If he's told you everything then I'm quite sure you don't need me to repeat it,' she said.

'So you admit you were in on the fraud?' asked Fisher.

She'd spoken carelessly. She should have denied all knowledge of it and pretended to be surprised.

She said nothing. It was probably better that way.

'Where were you on the night Edward Galloway died?' Fisher asked.

'What does that have to do with anything? I was at home.'

'Do you have an alibi?'

She thought for a moment. 'A neighbour would have seen me.'

'When we first met, you told me and my colleague, Mrs Peel, that you were last at the National Gallery about three weeks before Galloway died,' said Fisher.

'Mrs Peel? Is that her name? Is she a private detective too?'

'Please answer my question, Miss Curwen.'

'Yes. I did say that.'

'When we spoke to Georgina Miller, Galloway's secretary, she told us you called on him about a week before his death.'

'She must be mistaken.'

'So you last saw Galloway three weeks before he died?'

'Yes.'

'You weren't at the gallery on the night he died?'

'No. I was at home. I've told you that.' She was trying to remain calm but it was difficult. Each question made her more flustered. She took in a breath and tried to relax her shoulders. She needed to take control of the situation. 'Did Cecil White-Thomas tell you he and I are lovers?' she said.

A pause followed. Fisher raised his eyebrows and Graham scratched his temple. To her delight, the pair of them looked suitably uncomfortable.

'No he didn't,' said Graham eventually. 'Is that why he did everything you told him to?'

She laughed. 'I told him?'

'That's what he said,' said Fisher.

Vanessa shook her head in dismay. Was Cecil trying to pin everything on her?

'You do know Edward Galloway was murdered, don't you?' said Graham.

She stared at him for a moment, unsure if she'd heard correctly. 'He was murdered?' she said. 'Not a heart attack?'

'No it was poison.'

She looked down at the smooth polished wood grain in her desk. Had Cecil done it? Galloway had told him about the painting, *Portrait of a Widow with a Lark*. He'd said it was quite obvious the painting was forged. He even told Cecil he was astonished he hadn't noticed it himself.

Had Cecil poisoned him out of anger? A need to silence him?

The news it was murder had shaken her. She pulled out her cigarette case and Fisher appeared to notice her fingers trembling.

'Are you alright, Miss Curwen?'

'No,' she said. 'I'm not. I never thought Cecil would do something like this.'

Chapter Fifty-Three

Augusta listened as Philip recounted the interviews he'd conducted that day with Cecil White-Thomas and Vanessa Curwen.

'They both admitted to the forgery,' he said. 'Apparently, they worked on it together. And now they're each scrambling to blame the other. Classic strategy.' He paused, then added, 'It also turns out they were having a love affair.'

Augusta gasped. 'Really? I'm astonished. I'm also rather disappointed we didn't uncover that ourselves.'

'Miss Curwen was the one who confirmed it,' Philip said. 'And it certainly explains their close collaboration on the fake Veridiano. From what I gathered, they planned to split the profits. It was all very calculated.'

'I'm surprised they both confessed to the fraud so quickly. What about Galloway? Did they kill him?'

Philip shook his head. 'No. I don't think they did. They confessed to the fraud because both were keen to deny they had anything to do with Galloway's murder. Inspector Graham and I put the accusation to both of them quite directly. They were clearly shocked to learn he'd been poisoned.'

'They could be putting on an act,' Augusta said. 'They've already proven themselves convincing liars.'

'I don't deny that,' said Philip. 'They fooled half the art world with Veridiano. But when it came to Galloway's death, their reactions didn't feel rehearsed. There was a genuine surprise and shock. Graham's working now to verify their alibis for the night Galloway died.'

'And Ridley?' asked Augusta.

'Graham believes now the attack on Ridley really was just a robbery. Unconnected to Galloway's death.'

'So Scotland Yard is officially treating Galloway's death as murder now,' Augusta said. 'Wetherell won't be pleased about that, he wanted it all kept secret.'

'It was bound to happen,' said Philip. 'You can only keep a poisoning quiet for so long. Fortunately, Graham isn't pressing for a full Yard investigation yet. He's happy to keep it under his supervision for now. I explained the reasons for Wetherell's secrecy, and Graham is being accommodating.'

Augusta smiled. 'That's quite rare, isn't it? A Scotland Yard inspector choosing not to step in and seize control?'

'Are you implying the Yard likes to swoop in and take all the credit?'

'I didn't say that, Philip,' she responded. 'You did.'

He gave a gentle laugh and reached for his teacup. He sighed when he found it empty. 'I think this moment calls for something a little stronger,' he said, rising to his feet.

Augusta watched him cross the room to a cupboard behind his desk. He opened it, reached inside, and pulled out a bottle of whisky.

'I had no idea you kept that up here,' Augusta said.

'I like to keep it hidden. I don't make a habit of it, but

sometimes, when things get complicated, it helps to clear the fog.'

He poured two measures into short glasses and brought them over. Augusta accepted hers gratefully and settled back in her chair. The drink was warm and sharp, and she savoured the heat in her throat.

'If Galloway wasn't killed because of the forged painting,' she said, 'then it has to go back to his past. The war. His betrayal.'

Philip nodded slowly. 'Yes. That's where this leads.'

Augusta took another sip. 'So we need to return to the railway arch.'

He looked at her, his expression grim. 'Whatever answers remain... they're likely to be there.'

A long silence fell between them. Outside, a clock chimed the hour.

Chapter Fifty-Four

AUGUSTA AND PHILIP arrived at the railway arch early the following morning. Icy flakes fell from the slate grey sky as they left the tube station and hurried across Holloway Road.

Once inside the arch, they set to work looking through the remaining files. Augusta worked hurriedly, quickly passing over names and locations which didn't mean anything to her.

'I don't think there's anything more here,' she said to Philip after a while. 'I think it's time to look in the cupboards.'

'Very well.' Philip pushed the file he was looking through back into its drawer. 'I'll join you. I'm not finding much either.'

They shone their torch beams onto the steel cupboards which sat at the back of the room. A thin layer of grit from the brickwork had accumulated on top of them.

A train rumbled overhead as Augusta opened the first cupboard. Inside were several leather bags which looked familiar. 'Portable telephone sets,' she said once the train had passed. 'I didn't expect to see these again.' She pulled one out. 'I think this one might even be the one I used! I remember its case had a broken buckle like this one.' She put it back in its place, worried that if she held it too long some unwelcome memories would return. 'And first aid kits too.' She picked up one of the little boxes with a red cross marked on it. 'We all had these.'

Philip opened another cupboard. 'There's an old signal radio here. It looks remarkably like the one Lennox used. And these...' he pulled out a stack of notebooks tied together with string. 'They look like field reports.'

Augusta's beam caught something at the back of the cupboard. A section of rolled canvas. She retrieved it and unrolled it on the concrete floor. The painting was a serene landscape of a lake, its still surface reflecting dusky hills beneath an evening sunset.

'It's beautiful,' said Philip. 'One of Hastings' pictures?'

'I think it must be. He was very talented. But there was always more to his work, each painting was a map in disguise.'

'Can you see the clues?' Philip asked.

'I think so... the curve of the shoreline mimics the bend of the river. The jetty points to the railway crossing. And that heron must mark something, a storage depot perhaps. Hastings often placed animals in pictures to signify locations.'

'He was a brilliant man,' Philip said. 'But not a brave one. When it counted most, he chose himself. We were trained to know that might happen, that any of us might fall. But none of us expected betrayal from one of our own.'

With a bitter taste in her mouth, Augusta rolled up the painting and put it back in the cupboard.

'There's a bag in here,' said Philip. He pulled it out and

opened it. Augusta peered in to see a few small objects: a pocket watch, a silver comb and a broken pen.

'Who did this belong to?' she said.

'Look, there's a book too,' said Philip, pulling it out. It was a pocket edition of *The Jungle Book* by Rudyard Kipling. 'You're the book lady,' he said, handing it to her. 'You'll probably want to have a look at it.'

Augusta opened the book. The inside cover bore a name, faded but familiar. She smiled. 'Blake. I think I remember him reading this.' It seemed a shame such a personal item was sitting forgotten in a cupboard. 'This bag must have belonged to Blake,' she said. 'It doesn't belong here, it should be returned to his family.'

She turned to the back of the book and some folded papers fell out. As she picked them up, she recognised the feel of thin writing paper. 'Letters,' she said.

'Blake's letters?' asked Philip.

Augusta opened one. It was short and dated January 1917. '"My dear Edmund,"' she read. '"There was frost this morning, and I thought of your warm hands in mine. I've sewn your initials into my scarf. Keep warm, my love. Keep safe. Artemisia."'

'Artemisia?' said Philip. 'That's a pretty name. I don't recall Blake ever mentioning her.'

'We didn't talk much about that sort of thing, did we?' said Augusta. 'We couldn't share a lot of information about our lives back home. And besides... some of it felt too painful to talk about.'

Philip nodded. She read out another. '"The postman brought your letter and I held it to my lips before I opened it—does that sound silly? But your words made my heart lighter. Artemisia."'

They remained silent for a moment. Edmund Blake

had died young. The courtship with Artemisia would only have been short.

Augusta felt a heaviness in her chest as she thought about Edmund and Artemisia. When had they last seen each other?

When she spoke, her voice felt tight with emotion. 'I wonder what Artemisia is doing now?' she said. 'I can only hope she survived the war.'

'I hope so too,' said Philip.

Chapter Fifty-Five

LILLIAN GALLOWAY SAT at her father's desk, absently chewing the end of her pen. Her notebook lay open in front of her, the page blank. She was going to write her final poem about her father. But where to begin?

She glanced around the office. Books filled the shelves: volumes about old masters, the history of European art and faded exhibition catalogues. It had all meant so much to him. And yet, he'd always seemed unable to share his passion for art with her.

The door creaked open. She turned to see Miss Miller standing on the threshold, surprise on her face.

'Miss Galloway,' the secretary said. 'I didn't realise you were in here. I usually keep the office locked.'

'It was open,' Lillian replied. 'I just wanted to visit.'

'It was open?' Miss Miller stepped inside and gently closed the door behind her. 'Would you like a cup of tea? Coffee?'

'No, thank you. I'm not planning to stay long.'

Lillian set her pen down. She could feel the words for

her poem slipping further from reach. 'What will happen to this office?' she asked. 'Will someone else take it over?'

'I imagine so,' said Miss Miller. 'There's always a shortage of office space, and this one is... rather enviable.' She gave a faint smile, gesturing at the space and the large window. 'Please feel free to take anything that belonged to your father. Most of the books here were his personal copies.'

'I might take a few,' Lillian said. 'But the rest can stay. They're valuable resources. I'm sure someone else will make good use of them.'

Miss Miller nodded. 'Absolutely.'

Lillian hesitated. She'd told no one yet about what she'd found, or the secret it revealed. She had always imagined confronting her father directly, but the moment had slipped away, stolen by his sudden death. 'I discovered something about my father recently,' she said quietly.

Miss Miller's brow furrowed. 'What sort of something?'

'I think he might have been a spy,' Lillian said. 'During the war.'

The colour seemed to drain from Miss Miller's face. She crossed the room and slowly sat down in the chair opposite. 'A spy?'

Lillian nodded. 'He never told me. I didn't visit him very often. He left my mother and me when I was eleven. After that, I didn't want to see him. Sometimes he asked, and I said no. Sometimes I relented. I'd visit his flat. He had even more books there, he was always surrounded by them.'

Miss Miller remained still, listening closely.

'After my mother died, I went to live with her sister. I didn't get along with my aunt, so I started seeing my father more— weekends here and there. He tried to be kind, but there was always a distance between us. I wanted… something more. A real relationship. One where we could talk, be open. But every conversation felt like a struggle. I used to think it was my fault. Now I wonder if it was simply who he was.'

'I understand that,' Miss Miller said. 'He was thoughtful, but never easy to talk to.'

'During the war, he went away again. He told me he was in Canada and worked in a gallery there. I never questioned it. He was gone for a few years, and when he came back, I suppose I resented him for leaving again. Although this time it wasn't his choice. He had to go. But then I found something…'

'What did you find?'

Lillian reached into her satchel and drew out a worn identity card. She placed it carefully on the desk. 'I borrowed a book from my father recently. When I opened it at home, this fell out.'

Miss Miller leaned forward. Her eyes widened.

'My goodness. That's him. He looks younger, but yes, that's your father. How long ago was this?'

'The card says it was issued in 1916.'

'So it does.' She studied the card more closely. 'But this name… Jean-Marie Charpentier?'

'A false name,' said Lillian. 'It says he was an enseignant d'art. An art teacher.'

'And Belgian,' Miss Miller murmured. 'He passed for Belgian?'

Lillian shrugged. 'I can't imagine it. But apparently, he did. He lived undercover in Belgium. That was clearly his assignment. And I think I've met someone who worked with him there, his old friend Roger Parker.'

Miss Miller leaned back in her chair. 'Is that so?'

'Mr Parker told me he'd worked with my father in

Canada but I knew it had to be a lie. So Mr Parker must have worked undercover in the war too.'

'Goodness.' Miss Miller scratched her temple. 'I didn't realise that.' She fixed Lillian's gaze and gave her a sympathetic look. 'This discovery must have been quite a shock for you.'

Lillian nodded. 'It was. My father never told me much about his time in Canada and now I know why. He was having to concoct a lie. And perhaps he felt bad about that?' She shrugged. 'It's difficult to know.'

'And now you know what he really did,' said Miss Miller. 'And you can understand why he couldn't tell you the truth. He was serving his country like so many others. And pretending to be Belgian too. He must have been very brave.'

Lillian looked down at her blank page. 'I suppose he had to be at times.'

Miss Miller was quiet for a moment. Then she added, 'At least he came back.'

'Yes. He came back.'

'So many didn't.'

Chapter Fifty-Six

'THIS IS A LOVELY LITTLE BOOK,' said Fred later that afternoon, gently thumbing through the pocket-sized copy of *The Jungle Book*.

'Yes it is,' said Augusta. 'That's why I wanted to show it to you. I thought you'd appreciate it. I'm thinking of returning it to Edmund's family. It feels... right.'

Fred looked up, his brow furrowing. 'So Edmund's no longer—?'

'No,' Augusta said softly. 'He's gone.'

She paused, then continued, 'Edmund Blake was one of three agents Philip and I worked with in Belgium during the war. The others were Victor Lennox and Mabel Cavendish. Sadly, they're gone too. Philip and I recently gained access to an old storage unit in North London. Inside were files, equipment... and personal items from our unit during the war. That's where we found this.'

Fred set the book down with care. 'I'm sorry, Augusta,' he said gently. 'It must've been difficult to see it again.'

'It was.' She picked up the book and ran her fingers over the cover. 'But it brought Edmund back, in a way. I don't know who his family are, but I'll find out because I think they'd want this returned. It's something precious.' She opened the book, turning its pages slowly. Then she paused. 'There's something in here.'

A sliver of cream card, no bigger than an inch across, was tucked between the pages. She pulled it out.

It was a small photograph.

Fred leaned in. 'Who's that?'

The image showed a young woman with a direct gaze and a faint, knowing smile. Augusta turned the photograph over. Written on the back in slanted script were four simple words:

All my love, A xxx

She turned it back again, studying the woman's face.

'A,' she said. 'For Artemisia.'

Fred looked at her. 'Artemisia?'

Augusta nodded. 'And I've seen her somewhere before…'

Chapter Fifty-Seven

'WELL, I NEVER,' said Philip, studying the photograph in his hand. 'This is a surprise.'

'We need to move quickly,' said Augusta.

Philip glanced at the clock on the wall. 'Let's try Mr Sandford at *The Art Chronicle*. He's probably left for the day, but we'll do what we can. If we can't speak to him in person, a telephone call will have to do.' He put the photograph down on his desk and straightened. 'And then,' he added, 'we need to speak to Wetherell.'

'How?' said Augusta. 'He's not easily reachable. And he told us no one in Whitehall knows who he is.'

Philip gave a smile. 'Then maybe it's time to stop being polite. We go to the War Office, march in and make a bit of noise. If he's watching—as I suspect he is—word will get back to him. He won't be able to ignore us.' He turned to the telephone on his desk. 'I'll ring Inspector Graham at the Yard as well.'

'You're going to tell him?'

'Yes, Graham will help us. His men can move fast. Establishing alibis, checking records, that sort of thing. We need facts now. As many as we can gather.' He paused and looked at her. 'I know it's daunting, Augusta. But we're close now.'

She reached across his desk and squeezed his hand. 'I know,' she said. 'We're nearly there.'

Chapter Fifty-Eight

AUGUSTA AND PHILIP arrived at the National Gallery early the next morning with Inspector Graham in tow.

Augusta stifled a yawn as they climbed the cold, stone steps. She hadn't slept all night. And all she could do now was pray they'd got their facts right.

Georgina Miller got up from her desk as they entered the secretaries' office. 'Mr and Mrs Parker,' she said. 'You're back again?'

'Yes,' said Augusta. 'Although our names are Mrs Peel and Mr Fisher. We're private detectives. And with us here is Detective Inspector Graham of Scotland Yard.'

The young woman gasped, then eyed the inspector anxiously, biting her lip.

'Good morning, Miss Miller,' said Graham. 'Is there somewhere we can talk privately?'

By now the other secretaries in the room had stopped their work and were watching them.

'I'm not sure... Mr Galloway's office I suppose,' she said. 'What's this about?'

'We'll explain everything in a moment,' said the inspector.

A short while later, they gathered in Edward Galloway's office. The scene of his murder.

'Please take a seat, Miss Miller,' the inspector guided her to a chair. 'Make yourself comfortable.'

The secretary did so then stared at them in turn, eyes wide.

'Mrs Peel will do all the explaining,' said Graham, propping himself against Galloway's desk.

'Me?' said Augusta. 'Alright then.'

She turned to Miss Miller. The young woman looked afraid. Augusta felt rather sorry for her. 'We're not the only people who've been working under aliases. You've been doing the same. Your name isn't really Georgina Miller, is it?'

The secretary blanched. 'I don't know what you're talking about.'

Her hands fidgeted in her lap.

'You used to work on *The Art Chronicle* for the editor Mr Sandford,' continued Augusta. 'He has fond memories of you. He says you were a good worker. You left the publication to work here at the National Gallery. Three months ago, you were asked to be Edward Galloway's secretary.'

She nodded. 'That's true.'

'It had been your plan to become his secretary for a long time, hadn't it? You got the job at *The Art Chronicle* so you could gain secretarial experience in the art world. When a job at this gallery became available, you must have been delighted to secure it. And when Edward Galloway's previous secretary left... you'd achieved your goal.'

'Goal? I didn't have a goal.'

'I think you did,' said Augusta. 'Your goal was revenge.'

Miss Miller shook her head.

'Mr Fisher and I knew Edmund Blake quite well,' said Augusta.

The secretary's eyes widened at the mention of his name.

'We worked together in a small espionage network in occupied Belgium. Blake was a good man. He was brave, clever, and utterly loyal.'

A tear slipped down Miss Miller's cheek. She quickly brushed it away with her fingers.

'We also worked with an agent called Jonathan Hastings,' continued Augusta. 'A talented artist who hid maps in his paintings and had them smuggled back to Britain. After the war, Hastings returned to the art world and worked here in this gallery. He used his real name again, Edward Galloway. He was fortunate he returned from the war relatively unscathed. Especially after his capture in March 1917. Blake was also captured alongside two other agents. They were Victor Lennox and Mabel Cavendish. Hastings was released by the enemy, the other three were not so lucky.' She paused for a moment, trying to keep the emotion out of her voice. 'Mr Fisher and I discovered recently they'd been betrayed. Betrayed by Jonathan Hastings. He traded his life for theirs.'

Augusta waited for a reaction from Miss Miller, but none came. Instead, she bowed her head and looked at her hands.

'Your real name is Jane Christie, isn't it?' said Augusta. 'You worked as a secretary in military intelligence here in London. We know this because we paid a visit to the War Office last night. You and Edmund Blake were in love.'

She noticed Miss Miller's shoulders give way a little.

'You sent each other letters and you used the code

name Artemisia. We never would have worked out who Artemisia was if we hadn't found the photograph of you which Edmund kept in his copy of *The Jungle Book*.'

Miss Miller wiped her eyes.

'I can't imagine how awful it must have been for you when Edmund was captured,' said Augusta. 'And no doubt you were desperate to find out what had happened to him. Your position as a secretary in military intelligence allowed you to access files. You probably weren't allowed to, but you wanted answers. And you found them.'

A long pause followed. Miss Miller pulled a handkerchief from her pocket and wiped her face. Then she smoothed her skirt and looked up at Augusta.

'You'd have done the same,' she said.

'I don't know how I would have reacted,' said Augusta. 'But I do know I wouldn't have resorted to murder. We heard Galloway received threatening letters. Did you write them?'

Miss Miller nodded. 'I wanted him to feel frightened. I wanted him to be looking over his shoulder all the time, worried about who was coming for him.'

Augusta took in a breath. It was quite clear the secretary had been consumed by her resentment for the man.

'How did you know Jonathan Hastings was Edward Galloway?' Philip asked Miss Miller.

She paused before replying. 'I read an interview with him in *The Art Chronicle*,' she said. 'I didn't realise who he was until I saw his photograph. Then I recognised him. He came into the Whitehall office once, after he'd been released. He was so pleased with himself. He expected us all to give him a hero's welcome. But I couldn't... Not with Edmund still missing. I feared the worst. And then when I saw it confirmed in the file... my world fell apart.'

She put her handkerchief to her face as fresh tears

spilled down her cheeks. Augusta stepped away, feeling the need to allow her some privacy.

After a short while, Inspector Graham straightened himself and cleared his throat. 'Miss Miller. You told Mrs Peel and Mr Fisher that you visited your sister on the night of Mr Galloway's death. My men called on your sister.'

'Did they?' She looked up, surprised. 'What did she say?'

'Your sister and her husband confirmed you called on them that evening but said you left at half past seven. A security guard here at the gallery has confirmed you arrived here at eight o'clock that evening explaining you'd left something in your office which you needed to retrieve. During your time here that evening you called on Mr Galloway in this office and offered to make him a cup of coffee. You knew he regularly worked late into the evening, so you expected to find him here. Am I right?'

Miss Miller said nothing.

'Perhaps you'll tell us where you obtained the cyanide which you put in his coffee. But I know it's not too difficult. It can be bought to control rats or fumigate other pests. It's also used in the processing of photographs. I've no doubt you invented a legitimate explanation to get your hands on it. Once it was in his coffee, Mr Galloway stood no chance, did he? But in your eyes, he murdered your sweetheart. And so you took your revenge.'

Augusta's heart ached. Miss Miller had spent years planning murder. Her actions had been cold and calculating. She'd gone to great lengths to avenge her loved one's death.

But where had it got her?

Although Augusta felt pleased they'd solved the case, she also felt deep sympathy and sorrow.

Chapter Fifty-Nine

'I THINK Sparky wants to stretch his wings,' said the Dowager Lady Pontypool, peering into the canary's cage. 'Poor creature, so confined.'

'He doesn't mind it,' Augusta replied. 'He's quite content watching the customers come and go. And he flies about my flat each morning and evening.'

'But he had such a lovely time fluttering around the shop the other day, didn't he?' said Lady Pontypool, eyes twinkling.

'Oh yes,' said Lady Hereford. 'He loved every minute of it.'

'The only trouble was getting him back into his cage,' said Augusta. 'That took a long time.'

'That's because he needs more discipline,' declared Lady Pontypool. 'You must be firm with these little creatures. I've heard budgerigars can be very disobedient.'

'He's a canary,' Lady Hereford corrected.

'Oh, did I say budgerigar again? Silly me. I meant canary.'

Lady Hereford glanced at the Pomeranian dog in her friend's arms. 'What about Fifi?' she said. 'She's perfectly capable of walking, and yet you carry her everywhere.'

Lady Pontypool looked down at the little dog. 'She's nervous. And if I were her size, I'd want to be carried too. Still...' She glanced around the shop. 'Perhaps she might enjoy a little explore around here?'

'She probably wouldn't,' Augusta said hastily, recalling an out-of-control dog she once had in her shop.

'No, maybe not,' Lady Pontypool said. 'But she does like Russell Square. Perhaps we'll go there. It's cold, but sunny, and she could do with a bit of a scamper.'

'A splendid idea,' said Lady Hereford. She turned to her nurse. 'Doris, we're going to Russell Square. Fifi needs some exercise.'

Philip descended the stairs just as the two ladies were preparing to leave.

'Oh, hello, Mr Fisher—and goodbye!' Lady Hereford said. 'We're off to walk Fifi in the square. Would you care to join us?'

'That's very kind, but I'm a little busy,' Philip said.

'A dreadful shame,' sighed Lady Pontypool. 'And you're such a handsome chap, too.'

Philip cast an awkward glance at Augusta as the women left.

Augusta laughed. 'It's funny to think they're best friends now. Not long ago Lady Hereford was complaining bitterly about her lifelong adversary.'

'People can be fickle,' said Philip.

'So what are you actually busy with?' Augusta asked.

'Nothing at all,' he said, smiling. 'I simply didn't fancy trailing behind two ladies and a pampered dog. I'd much rather spend time with you.'

'That's very nice of you,' Augusta said. 'It's been such a busy few weeks—we haven't really had a chance to do anything enjoyable.'

'Maybe not. But I enjoy working with you, Augusta.'

She smiled. 'And this time we managed it without too many arguments. That bodes well for the future.'

The future. The phrase lingered. She wanted to ask Philip about his plans for his divorce, but as always, something held her back. Perhaps things were best left as they were. She and Philip had independent lives but they enjoyed shared moments together too. It was a balance which seemed to work at the moment.

'Owen Ridley's out of hospital,' Philip said. 'Recovering well, apparently.'

'That's good news,' said Augusta. 'Do you think he was involved in the Veridiano forgery?'

Philip shook his head. 'I don't think he knew about it. Inspector Graham's working on the case. It turns out Vanessa Curwen put the forged sketchbooks into the box Ridley had bought at auction. They weren't even part of the lot. She planted them afterwards, during a visit to his shop.'

'And the paintings which appeared in house clearances and the church?'

'Graham has discovered Curwen and Cecil-White had connections to the places. They knew people in each location and managed to gain access to hide a painting. The pair of them were rather clever. They pulled off quite a deception, didn't they? Their reputations gave them cover. People believed them because of who they were.'

'And because they were so well regarded, they assumed they'd never be questioned,' said Augusta. 'But they weren't as clever as they thought. White-Thomas didn't even bother destroying the practice papers he used to test his ageing technique. And if another expert had examined the sketchbooks, the forgery would have soon been uncovered. I don't think Curwen and White-Thomas were clever at all. In fact, I think they're the most dangerous type of people. Those who believe they're far cleverer than they actually are.'

'That probably covers most criminals,' Philip said with a smile.

'And Georgina Miller?' Augusta asked. 'Any word on how she's faring?'

'Graham says she's made a full confession. I find it hard to blame her. What Hastings did was unforgivable. If I'd known back then that he'd betrayed our comrades… I don't know what I'd have done…'

'I understand her reasoning too,' said Augusta. 'But revenge doesn't bring peace. Lillian Galloway has lost her father. Nothing can change that.'

'No,' said Philip quietly. He glanced towards the shop window. 'I can see why the two ladies went for a walk. It's a beautiful afternoon. We haven't had many like this.' He turned to her. 'Do you fancy a stroll?'

'Yes,' Augusta said with a smile. 'I think I do.'

Once they'd fetched their hats and coats, they stepped out into the autumnal afternoon. Augusta slipped her arm through Philip's and, for a moment, they walked in silence.

Then she spoke. 'The war ended years ago,' she said. 'But it's never quite released us, has it?'

'Not really. It will always be there.'

'Like a ghost.'

'Yes. Like a ghost. But it can only haunt us if we let it, Augusta. Life has moved on in so many other ways.

Ahead of them on the street, Augusta could see the Dowager Lady Pontypool walking alongside Lady Hereford's bath chair and nurse.

She watched them for a moment—rivals turned companions—and felt a quiet hope. Life, she thought, always finds a way to surprise.

'Come on,' she said to Philip. 'Let's see where this afternoon takes us.'

And together, they walked on.

Chapter Sixty

AROUND THREE MILLION people visit London's National Gallery each year. The gallery is housed in a grand neoclassical building overlooking Trafalgar Square and Admiral Nelson on his famous column.

The gallery was established in 1824 with a collection of paintings acquired from the estate of John Julius Angerstein—a Russian-born British businessman and avid art collector. His private collection was purchased for the nation and initially displayed at his former home, 100 Pall Mall.

In 1838, the Gallery moved to its current site in Trafalgar Square. The new building, hampered by limited funds and an awkwardly shaped plot, was met with criticism at the time of its opening. Despite these early challenges, the building has evolved over the years through various extensions and improvements. The original façade remains unchanged and is now considered one of London's most cherished landmarks.

During the Second World War, as bombing raids threatened the capital, many of the gallery's most valuable paintings were evacuated to safe locations in Wales—including storage deep within a disused slate mine.

Tiziano Vecellio, better known as Titian, was a leading figure of the Italian Renaissance and one of the most influential painters of the 16th century. One of his most celebrated works, *Venus and Adonis*, exists in around thirty known versions—many produced with the help of his studio assistants.

Scholars continue to debate which version can be considered the definitive or 'final' one. The version held by London's National Gallery dates to 1554 and was part of the original collection acquired from John Julius Angerstein.

Holloway Road tube station opened in 1906 and is one of many striking London Underground stations designed by architect Leslie Green. As architect for the Underground Electric Railways Company of London in the early 20th century, Green created a distinctive architectural style known as Modern Style (British Art Nouveau), first seen in the 1880s.

His station designs are easily recognised by their deep oxblood red glazed tiles and elegant semi-circular windows. Green was commissioned to design fifty stations, many of which still stand today as iconic features of London's transport network. His legacy is all the more remarkable given that he died in 1908 at the age of just thirty-three.

The railway arches opposite Holloway Road tube station once supported a bridge which has since been dismantled. This spot was once a busy crossing point for multiple railway lines linked to the Great Northern Railway. Trains from King's Cross passed overhead, along with routes serving local sidings and the vast St Pancras goods depot.

Today, the sidings and the depot are long gone, but a few of the original lines remain in use as part of the London North Eastern Railway network.

Bloomsbury Square, the location of Vanessa Curwen's gallery, is one of the oldest garden squares in London, It was originally laid out in the 17th century and was a fashionable address for the upper classes. By the 19th century, it had become a predominantly middle-class neighbourhood and underwent significant rebuilding during this period.

Among its notable residents was a young Benjamin Disraeli who later became prime minister. Over the years, many of the square's elegant houses have been converted into offices.

The End

Historical Note

Around three million people visit London's National Gallery each year. The gallery is housed in a grand neo-classical building overlooking Trafalgar Square and Admiral Nelson on his famous column.

The gallery was established in 1824 with a collection of paintings acquired from the estate of John Julius Angerstein—a Russian-born British businessman and avid art collector. His private collection was purchased for the nation and initially displayed at his former home, 100 Pall Mall.

In 1838, the Gallery moved to its current site in Trafalgar Square. The new building, hampered by limited funds and an awkwardly shaped plot, was met with criticism at the time of its opening. Despite these early challenges, the building has evolved over the years through various extensions and improvements. The original façade remains unchanged and is now considered one of London's most cherished landmarks.

During the Second World War, as bombing raids threatened the capital, many of the gallery's most valuable

Historical Note

paintings were evacuated to safe locations in Wales—including storage deep within a disused slate mine.

Tiziano Vecellio, better known as Titian, was a leading figure of the Italian Renaissance and one of the most influential painters of the 16th century. One of his most celebrated works, *Venus and Adonis*, exists in around thirty known versions—many produced with the help of his studio assistants.

Scholars continue to debate which version can be considered the definitive or 'final' one. The version held by London's National Gallery dates to 1554 and was part of the original collection acquired from John Julius Angerstein.

Holloway Road tube station opened in 1906 and is one of many striking London Underground stations designed by architect Leslie Green. As architect for the Underground Electric Railways Company of London in the early 20th century, Green created a distinctive architectural style known as Modern Style (British Art Nouveau), first seen in the 1880s.

His station designs are easily recognised by their deep oxblood red glazed tiles and elegant semi-circular windows. Green was commissioned to design fifty stations, many of which still stand today as iconic features of London's transport network. His legacy is all the more remarkable given that he died in 1908 at the age of just thirty-three.

The railway arches opposite Holloway Road tube station once supported a bridge which has since been dismantled. This spot was once a busy crossing point for multiple railway lines linked to the Great Northern Railway. Trains from King's Cross passed overhead, along with

Historical Note

routes serving local sidings and the vast St Pancras goods depot.

Today, the sidings and the depot are long gone, but a few of the original lines remain in use as part of the London North Eastern Railway network.

Bloomsbury Square, the location of Vanessa Curwen's gallery, is one of the oldest garden squares in London, It was originally laid out in the 17th century and was a fashionable address for the upper classes. By the 19th century, it had become a predominantly middle-class neighbourhood and underwent significant rebuilding during this period.

Among its notable residents was a young Benjamin Disraeli who later became prime minister. Over the years, many of the square's elegant houses have been converted into offices.

Thank you

Thank you for reading this Augusta Peel mystery, I really hope you enjoyed it!

Would you like to know when I release new books? Here are some ways to stay updated:

- Like my Facebook page: facebook.com/emilyorganwriter
- Follow me on Goodreads: goodreads.com/emily_organ
- Follow me on BookBub: bookbub.com/authors/emily-organ
- View my other books here: emilyorgan.com

And if you have a moment, I would be very grateful if you would leave a quick review online. Honest reviews of my books help other readers discover them too!

Also by Emily Organ

Penny Green Series:

Limelight
The Rookery
The Maid's Secret
The Inventor
Curse of the Poppy
The Bermondsey Poisoner
An Unwelcome Guest
Death at the Workhouse
The Gang of St Bride's
Murder in Ratcliffe
The Egyptian Mystery
The Camden Spiritualist

Penny Green and Emma Langley Series:

The Whitechapel Widow
The Poison Puzzle

Also by Emily Organ

Churchill & Pemberley Series:

Tragedy at Piddleton Hotel
Murder in Cold Mud
Puzzle in Poppleford Wood
Trouble in the Churchyard
Wheels of Peril
The Poisoned Peer
Fiasco at the Jam Factory
Disaster at the Christmas Dinner
The Teapot Killer
Christmas Calamity at the Vicarage (novella)

Writing as Martha Bond

Lottie Sprigg Travels Mystery Series:

Murder in Venice
Murder in Paris
Murder in Cairo
Murder in Monaco
Murder in Vienna

Lottie Sprigg Country House Mystery Series:

Murder in the Library
Murder in the Grotto
Murder in the Maze
Murder in the Bay

Made in the USA
Las Vegas, NV
28 June 2025

24198711R00152